THE BILLIONAIRE CINDERELLA TEST

BILLIONAIRE ONLINE DATING SERVICE BOOK #2

ELLE JAMES

TWISTED PAGE INC

THE BILLIONAIRE CINDERELLA TEST

BILLIONAIRE ONLINE DATING SERVICE BOOK #2

New York Times & *USA Today*
Bestselling Author

ELLE JAMES

Ebook ISBN: 978-1-62695-017-7

Print ISBN: 978-1-62695-018-4

Hearts can heal and dreams can come true, if you open your-self to the possibilities...

Elle James

AUTHOR'S NOTE

Enjoy other books by Elle James

Visit ellejames.com for more titles and release dates
For hot cowboys, visit her alter ego Myla Jackson at
mylajackson.com
and join Elle James and Myla Jackson's Newsletter at
http://ellejames.com/ElleContact.htm

CHAPTER 1

"WE GOT A PROBLEM, BOSS."

Gage Tate clenched his teeth and held his temper. "What now?"

"The replacement boom we contracted didn't show up this morning."

Not good. Of all days for work on the Platinum Towers to grind to a halt, now was not a good one. "Did you call and find out why?"

Marcus Shipley nodded. "Yup. He said he didn't have one available until a week from today."

"And when was he going to tell us?"

Marcus's lips twisted around the toothpick that had replaced cigarettes in his mouth. "A week from today."

"We can't come to a complete halt for an entire week. The delay on materials acquisition already set us two weeks behind schedule. Every day we go past our completion date costs us money."

"I have a call into another boom company; they

think they can get one to us in two days. My contact said he'd let us know by the end of the day."

"Great. I have a meeting with Mr. Langley in exactly," he glanced at his watch, "ten minutes. Here. To show him what we're capable of. On a work site where no work is being done." Gage raked a hand through his hair.

"William Langley? The man who owns half of downtown Dallas?"

"Yes. That Langley. I want that property on the corner of Elm and Griffin Streets."

"I thought he didn't want to sell it to you on account of you hadn't paid your dues."

"I have to convince him I wasn't handed my money. I earned every last damn cent, unlike so many of his cronies." He glanced at the parking area, wishing he had time to call in a crew to at least look like they were busy making progress on the multi-million-dollar project slipping further and further behind.

Marcus's eyes widened. "Ain't that the lady you hired to improve your image?"

Gage followed his nod toward the woman in a pencil skirt marching toward him with purpose in her stride, even if she couldn't quite lengthen her stride in that ridiculous skirt.

Marcus tipped his head down, hiding his grin from the woman advancing on them. "How's that going for you?'

"What?" Gaged stalled, hating that he'd had to hire an image consultant in order to secure the desired property. "She thinks I'm too unapproachable. That I need to soften up and or get laid."

Marcus grinned. "That's my kind of consultant. Think she'd go for someone like me?"

"No." Gage braced himself for Haddie Madison, the fifty-year-old image consultant he'd hired out of desperation. Pasting on his most congenial face, he greeted her with a forced smile. "What brings you out to the job site, Ms. Madison?"

Her brows twisted. "Wow. That's the best you can do? I can see straight through that pathetic attempt at pleasantries. And, please, call me Haddie."

Gage abandoned the fake smile. "Haddie. What are you doing here?"

"You said you had a meeting with Mr. Langley today, in ten minutes, if I'm not mistaken."

"Eight."

She nodded. "I'm here for moral support and to observe your interaction with the man."

Marcus coughed to hide his snort of laughter.

Gage glared at him. "Get your crew busy on something, even if it's only cleaning up the work site."

Marcus let loose his grin and clapped a hand to Gage's back, nearly knocking him over. "And that's why you're paid the big bucks, my friend." The site foreman strolled away whistling. Not a care in the world, other than finding a boom to replace the one that had crapped out on them on the tenth floor of a ninety-story project.

"Ah, that must be Mr. Langley now." Haddie turned toward the limousine easing into the job site.

"If you're going to be here, you need to wear a hard hat." Gage reached into his work truck where he kept spares and handed her a scuffed, yellow hard hat.

Haddie sighed. "And I just had my hair done."

Despite the damage to her hair, she settled the hat on her head and waited for the passenger of the limousine to alight.

Gage sucked in a deep breath. Nothing had gone right that morning. The boom hadn't arrived, Haddie had descended on him without warning and Langley had showed up on time. What more could go wrong?

The chauffeur parked, got out and opened the back door of the limousine and a bright turquoise blue stiletto emerged, followed by a long slender leg.

Gage groaned as Priscilla Langley unfolded her body from the back of the limo, flinging her long black hair back over her shoulder. Her father followed.

And that was what more could go wrong.

He'd invited Langley to the job site hoping to prove to the man he knew what he was doing and was capable of converting the man's eyesore of a building in downtown Dallas into a modern, designer structure that would bring more jobs and revenue to the city center. If only he'd leave his pain-in-the-ass daughter out of the equation.

Priscilla wobbled across the uneven gravel in her spike heels. "Gage, darling, I hope you don't mind, but Daddy insisted I come along." She held out her hand, her wrist limp like a queen expecting her subject to kiss her hand.

William Langley shook his head. "That's not how I remember it."

Gage gripped her hand and gave it a quick, firm shake. "Ms. Langley," he said, his lips stiff. He didn't need the drama of Langley's daughter distracting William from the reason he'd been invited there. When

4

he released his hold on Priscilla's hand, she didn't let go of his.

Forced to peel her fingers off his, Gage finally shook loose and held out his hand to William Langley. "Mr. Langley, thank, you for coming out to the job site."

Haddie cleared her throat, a slight frown pinching her brow for a second before she extended her hand. "Hello, Mr. Langley, Haddie Madison. I'm Mr. Tate's consultant."

William smiled and shook her hand. "What kind of consultant might that be?"

Gage held his breath, waiting for Haddie to spill the beans about his attempt to woo the great William Langley.

"Design consultant.," she said, her brows rising as she stared across at Gage. "I want this project to be the best it can be."

"This place is amazing." Priscilla walked toward the construction site. "Do you go up on those steel beams?"

Gage grabbed two hard hats from the back seat of his truck, handing one to William and hurrying after Priscilla with the other. "Ms. Langley, you have to wear a hard hat on the site."

She waved her manicured nails at him. "I don't need that. I never wear them on my father's work sites, do I, Daddy?" She smiled and blew a kiss at her father.

William Langley sighed. "I can't get her to do anything she doesn't want to do."

Gage held out the hat to the spoiled socialite. "Wear the hat or you'll have to stay in the limousine while we tour the site. I lose my liability insurance if anyone on the job site isn't wearing a hard hat."

Priscilla's pretty brow dented and her red painted lips pursed. "Daddy?"

Her father shrugged. "You can wait in the car if you don't want to mess up your hair."

"But I wanted to see what Gage is working on." She leaned into Gage and ran her fingers up the front of his shirt. "And to see if he has a date to his charity ball." She winked up at him, curling her fingers around his neck. "Do you?"

Anger burned a path from Gage's gut all the way up into his cheeks and threatened to explode out of the top of his head.

Haddie touched his arm and whispered, "Remember our project?"

The older woman's reminder clamped a lid on Gage's temper and he drew in a deep breath, untangled Priscilla's hands from around his neck and he said, "I'm sorry, I have a date to the charity ball. And since you don't want to wear your hat, I'm asking that you stay in the car while your father and I discuss business." There. He'd been as polite as he could be with a woman whose type he knew all too well and wanted none of.

Been to that rodeo, didn't want to ride that bull again.

Priscilla pouted and stared at the hard hat. "I'll wait in the car." She spun on her stilettos and stalked across the gravel, wobbling as she went.

Gage breathed in and out through his nostrils before turning to Mr. Langley. "Would you like to see what we're working on?" He fully expected the man to follow his daughter off the site and that would mean kissing goodbye Gage's chance to purchase the downtown property he'd been after for over a year.

Langley's gaze followed his daughter all the way to the limousine. When he turned, he smiled. "Yes. I'm here to see what you're capable of, and so far, I'm impressed."

Gage led Mr. Langley and Haddie through the site, showed them the drawings and talked about what he was most passionate about, building beautiful buildings that touched the sky.

When Langley departed, Haddie stood beside Gage, her eyes narrowing. "Yup. You have a long way to go on your manners with the ladies, Mr. Tate."

"I can't allow anyone on my site without a hard hat." Period. Gage crossed his arms. "If the hat wasn't a rule, I would have had to ban her from the site because of her open-toed shoes."

Haddie stared at Gage. "What is it about women you don't like, Mr. Tate?"

Everything, he wanted to say, but opted for, "Nothing." Other than they were gold-diggers, looking for the best deal in husband material.

For a long moment, Haddie paused, her gaze raking over him, making him want to squirm like a kid caught smoking in the restroom at school. "Well, Mr. Tate, you have to work with me if you want to shake the image of a cold-hearted son-of-a-bitch the media has labeled you as."

"I'm not cold-hearted," he grumbled, wishing the woman would leave and let him get back to what he did best—making something of nothing.

"The charity ball you'll be throwing will be the place you can change public opinion." Haddie crossed her arms. "But only if you treat women with respect and soften some of those rough edges."

"Why do I even have to go? The goal is to raise money for the charity. The rich and ridiculous will be there spending their money. I don't need to be there."

Haddie poked a finger at his chest. "If you want to sway Mr. Langley to sell you that property, you have to appear, even if you aren't, like a reasonable, caring man. You can't do that by hiding in your penthouse apartment."

He disliked parading in front of a bunch of society men and women who couldn't care less about him but were very interested in the money he could donate to all their causes. Where were the real people? "I hate wearing a damn tux."

"Tough." Haddie poked her finger at his chest again. "You just told a whopping lie to a woman who could convince her daddy that he shouldn't sell his property to you. And unless you want her to call you out on your lie, I suggest you find a suitable date for the charity ball and do it soon." Haddie handed him the hardhat and left.

Gage groaned. Where was he going to find a date for the ball that was only a couple weeks away? He absolutely refused to date a money-hungry socialite. Haddie was right, he did have a problem with women. Especially the kind that strung you along, claiming to love you when all they were interested in was being with the man with the most money. In Gage's book, they were all like that.

His cell phone beeped in his back pocket. He yanked

it out and glanced down, groaning again at the text from his friend Tag Bronson.

Billionaires Anonymous Club. Thirty minutes. Be there.

Gage texted, *Too busy.*

Sick? Tag responded.

No

Dying?

Gage sighed and keyed, *No.*

No excuses. We made a promise. Be there!

THIRTY MINUTES LATER...

IF HE'D THOUGHT his morning couldn't get worse, it most certainly could.

"Don't leave love up to luck. Like I told you the first time we met, with the help of my firm and heavily tested computer algorithms, you have a ninety-nine point nine percent chance of finding your perfect match. So, who's next?"

Leslie Lamb, the woman dressed in a soft gray suit, her blond, shoulder-length hair swinging, turned from the video screen to face the group of men seated around the conference table. On the screen was a picture of the first couple to find success through the Billionaire Online Dating System, or BODS as it was shortened to. Frank Cooper Johnson and his BODS match, Emma Jacobs.

Gage tapped his fingertips against the conference table surrounded by members of the Billionaires Anonymous Club, frankly amazed at how the first test of BODS had turned out. Who knew a computer program could pick the perfect match for one of their own? It had to be a lucky coincidence. Computers couldn't account for all the human traits and personality quirks.

But Cooper sat back with the biggest grin on his face, happier than a pig in mud.

So happy, Gage shifted in his seat, an itch crawling across his skin. No man could be that in love. Could he? Didn't he know what would eventually happen? No union lasted these days.

The men had formed the club back when they were five broke college students struggling to get an education at Texas A&M. On their last dime, and facing the distinct possibility of expulsion for various reasons—the most pressing reason having to do with money—they'd made a pact that they'd all become millionaires by the time they turned thirty. They'd formed a plan, stuck with it, finished college, each becoming, not millionaires, but billionaires by age thirty and achieving all their goals.

All except one. The one about getting married and raising a family. They'd all struggled with that one.

A year ago, Gage thought he'd be the first out the chute for the marriage goal. He'd been dating Lacy Welch, a beautiful blond who claimed to be crazy about him. She'd told him she loved him and he'd believed her. In the back of his mind he had images of the family-life some of his friends had grown up with—kids running around the yard, mothers kissing their babies good-night. For a brief moment in his ambitious drive to the top, he'd paused, thinking this was his chance. Until he'd proposed to Lacy, asking her to marry him and start a family together.

Boy had he been wrong.

She'd been horrified he'd wanted her to actually bear children. Lacy wanted the marriage without the family, afraid having children would destroy her figure and keep her from traveling the world. If he could promise her no children and an unlimited expense account, she'd marry him.

His ideal shattered, Gage ultimately figured he'd dodged a bullet. He retracted his proposal and went back to work, marriage no longer part of his equation for success.

"Ah, come on guys. It's not that bad." Cooper pulled Emma into his lap. "You heard the lady, I found my perfect match using BODS."

Gage shifted in his seat, ready for this meeting to be over. He had real issues to work through, like finding a date for the charity ball.. "Leslie, you have to change the acronym. BODS might send the wrong signals."

"Sorry, I have too much invested in letterhead, business cards and promo items to change it now." She winked at him.

"Just because it worked for Coop, doesn't mean it'll work for the rest of us." Gage drummed his fingers on the smooth surface of the mahogany conference table. "Sounds to me more like a crap shoot." He leaned back against his seat, ready to tune out of the rest of the conversation.

"You won't know until you give it a try." Taggert Bronson stepped up beside Leslie. "Gage, you have a charity ball coming up in a couple weeks, don't you?"

Gage snapped forward, the ball already making his stomach twist into a knot. He didn't need to bring it to the attention of the rest of his friends. "Yeah, so?"

"Why don't you give the system a shot and take the match it finds you. What's it gonna hurt? At the very least, you'll have a date for the ball."

Gage bristled, hating being the one on the spot for the hair-brained scheme. "Who said I didn't already have a date?"

Tag pinned him with a stare. "Do you?"

Gage thought through all the women he knew for a quick answer, someone he wouldn't mind asking to the ball and solve his problem with having lied to Priscilla. Unfortunately, most of his go-to girls ran in her circle. They might let slip that his invitation had been at the last minute, and if one of them did, his goose would be cooked with Daddy. "Damn it, no."

Sean O'Leary leaned over and nudged his arm. "I'm sure Priscilla Langley or Marilynn Tisdale would love to be your date. You could ask one of them. Maybe both."

"Hell, no." Gage sat up straight, staring across the boardroom table to Leslie. "Do the women you have signing up for this system know they're signing up to be matched with a wealthy man?"

Leslie shook her head. "Not at all. Some of them have money of their own and don't feel a need to marry well. Others may not have the kind of money you gentlemen have, but they are good people with sound ethics and values." She tipped her chin up. "I hand-select all the applicants for my system to ensure honesty and strong moral fiber."

Maxwell Smithson snorted. "Well, that rules us out."

Sean, Tag and Cooper laughed.

Gage didn't, his mind spinning with the possibility of finding a woman he could feel comfortable with to take to that confounded charity ball. "Can I get a woman who's down to earth? I'm sick to death of society debutantes and women who are only interested in the size of a man's bank account."

Leslie held her hand up like she was swearing in at court. "No fortune hunters or debutantes are allowed. Give my system a chance. I promise not all women are after money. Most just want to be treated nicely and maybe find love."

"I'm not looking for love or happily ever after. But I *could* use a date for the ball." He rubbed his chin. A woman unknown to the social elite of Dallas would be good. At least Priscilla wouldn't have any way of knowing he hadn't asked her to the ball until after he'd told Priscilla he had a date. And going through with BODS would get the other guys off his back.

"I'm still not believing you're throwing a ball in the first place," Sean commented. "I thought you hated that kind of event."

Gage grimaced. "Trust me. I'd rather slit my throat. Blame it on my image consultant. She insisted I throw one to demonstrate to the public I have a goddamn heart."

Sean laughed. "You mean it's not obvious to the media that our buddy, Gage Tate, has a heart of gold? What was it the news called you? Heartless, calculating and...what was the other adjective?"

Cooper, Maxwell and Tag answered as one, "Cutthroat."

"Yeah, yeah." Gage glared around the table. "Go ahead and laugh. You're not the one having to show up and smile for the cameras. Most of you are still anonymous." He focused on Leslie again, the notion of finding a date for the ball through BODS no longer completely appalling. "My name has been in the media too much lately. Is it possible to use a different name in your system to find a match?"

Leslie's brows dipped. "That would be dishonest."

"He's right." Tag tapped his chin. "Gage Tate would be an immediate giveaway."

Sean leaned toward the table. "Why not use your first name?"

"Austin?" Gage considered.

"Sure." Tag grinned. "No one associates Austin Tate with Gage Tate, Texas's most eligible bachelor. And it wouldn't be dishonest since it *is* your name."

Gage lifted the monogrammed pen in front of him and flipped it between his fingers, thinking. Haddie had been pushing him to ask one of the daughters of the charity matrons as a sign of good will. If he had a date already lined up for the event, he'd be off the hook. He wouldn't be pressured into escorting a society princess to an event he already dreaded as much as going to the dentist. "Okay." He inhaled and let it out slowly. "I'll do it. But I want to test her out first."

Max chuckled. "You're not taking a car for a test drive."

"In a way, I am." Gage didn't do anything without doing his homework first. He wouldn't be where he was today if he left things to chance. Not since Lacy, anyway. He refused to be humiliated like that, ever again. "I want to know that she's genuine and down to earth, but not so much of a redneck that she can't perform in public."

Emma's eyes narrowed. "I get it. You want a kind of Cinderella test."

Gage stared at Emma. "What?"

"You know." Emma leaned forward. "You want someone who is comfortable dusting furniture or mowing her own lawn, but who can also pull off wearing a dress and smiling in public. You don't want someone who will embarrass you."

"Yeah, I guess," Gage frowned, figuring Emma must think he was a complete jerk. "Hey, we're talking about a ball, not the rest of my damn life. Whomever I take can't be intimidated by the high-rollers who'll be there. I wouldn't want her feeling uncomfortable."

Emma nodded. "Of course. Still you don't want a woman who lets the pretty dress and fancy car go to her head."

"Yeah. I've had my fill of Priscilla Tisdales and Marilyn Langleys." He mentally added Lacy Welch to that list.

"You got them backwards. That's Priscilla Langley and Marilyn Tisdale," Sean corrected. "Although, either one of those women know what to wear and say in front of the big shots of Dallas."

Coop snorted. "They ought to, they've been groomed since birth to marry rich."

Gage shuddered at the thought of taking Priscilla or Marilyn to anything. "Can't stand either of those women. Plastic all the way through. Do they still make women who aren't only interested in money?"

Emma snorted. "We're not all money-hungry."

Gage turned to Leslie. "Seriously, do you have one of those?"

"I don't like the way this conversation is going." Emma Jacobs climbed out of Frank's lap and shook her head. "Whoever the system pulls out of the hat, you need to remember she's a real, live person with feelings. Frankly, all this talk is lacking in class and humility."

"Right," Leslie added. "This is a matchmaking application, but the people on both ends of the match are just that—people with emotions and feelings. I won't have anyone mistreated. Do you understand?"

"I do." Gage stood. "But also understand, that I'm a busy man with little time to waste on a dead end. If the woman doesn't work out, there's not second date and I'll have to find someone else to go with to the ball."

Leslie's lips pressed together. "Maybe you're not ready for my online dating system."

Gage's cheeks burned. He knew he was being a jerk but, damn it, he didn't want to go to the ball in the first place. In the second place, he really didn't have time to find a date. Having Leslie call him out on his rude behavior didn't sit well with him either.

"Look, I've agreed to do it. When do we start?" Once he'd set his mind on something, Gage rarely turned back.

"Don't worry." Tag patted Leslie's arm. "He's all bark, no bite."

"Yeah," Cooper said. "We'll make sure he does right by whomever he's matched with."

"Guys, I'm in the room," Gage bit out. "Let's do this before I change my mind."

"Right. You only have two weeks before the big to do." Max said.

Sean grinned. "You'll need time to find and test drive your new ride."

"You did *not* just say that." Emma shook her head and gave Gage a pointed look. "Don't hurt the girl."

Gage raised his hand. "I swear, I'll do my best not to. If all fails, I'll let her down easy." Which was more than he could say for how Lacy had smashed his idiotic dreams.

Leslie hesitated a moment longer, her gaze studying him for the longest.

Gage didn't know he'd been holding his breath until she gave a nod.

Her gaze remained narrowed. "Okay then, step into my office and I'll have you to fill out the online profile and preferences."

"So, *you're* the next guinea pig." Cooper rose and clapped a hand to Gage's back. "As someone said to me not long ago, *You won't regret it.*"

For a man known to be as cool as granite and just as hard to break, Gage's stomach churned and his palms sweat as he sat at Leslie's computer, entering his life story and the laundry list of requirements for his dream girl. As with all his undertakings, he was thorough.

He closed his eyes as he pushed ENTER, praying this wouldn't end up being a really bad mistake.

CHAPTER 2

WE COULD LOSE THE RANCH.

Fiona reeled from the news her father had told her that morning.

How could that be?

And then he'd told her not to worry about it. Go meet with her friend in Dallas. Too shocked to think straight, Fiona let her stepsisters, Bianca and Britney, talk her into keeping her lunch date with Leslie Lamb that day in Dallas. Did they understand how much it cost in gas alone to go back and forth from Temptation to Dallas in their father's old truck? It practically inhaled gas, then spewed it out in choking smoke from faulty gaskets. She'd have to get her brother, Magnus, to look into it. Maybe it was something easily fixed with little investment in parts.

"I can't wait to see Leslie. It's been ages since we all attended grief counseling with her," Britney gushed as they entered the office building where Leslie rented space.

Fiona checked the display board for the floor and suite number of BODS, the acronym for Leslie's new business.

"I can't wait to find out what fabulous new business she's started. " Bianca added, "I'll bet it's some kind of body shaping program, like medical weight loss or a yoga studio. I wonder if she needs an assistant."

"I thought you and Britney were going to start your own beauty shop," Fiona said.

Britney snorted. "Bianca's afraid of color."

"I'm not afraid of color." Bianca's shoulders sagged. "I'm afraid of messing up someone's hair *with* color."

"Same thing."

Fiona shook her head. "Aren't you two going to state board in two months?"

"Supposed to, but we're not sure Dad can afford the testing and licensing fees."

"Have you thought of maybe getting a job to pay for them yourselves?"

Britney rolled her eyes, ever the drama queen. "We're going to beauty school so that we can *get* jobs. Right now we're not qualified to do anything."

"You could wait tables or answer phones as a receptionist," Fiona suggested. "There *are* such things as staffing agencies that use people on a full or part time basis."

"Not many temp jobs going around in Temptation. We'd have to come all the way to Dallas for something like that."

Fiona stepped into the elevator and pushed the button for the tenth floor. She'd only been home for a couple days. She'd just graduated from Texas Tech in

Lubbock after putting herself through school, on the extended plan, working full time and going to school part time. She'd paid for her own room and board for the past two years to finish up her degree. But she'd done it.

Now all she had to do was find a job in Temptation or Hole in the Wall, close enough to help her dad with the ranch. He'd been on his own since she'd been gone. Magnus lived in Temptation and had his own business to run and only got out to the ranch twice a month to help their father with the bigger tasks. Neither Bianca nor Britney had shown an interest in ranching or taking care of the animals, and her father hadn't forced them to help outside, like he'd made Fiona and Magnus from a very young age.

The girls had been okay taking over all of the inside chores, but one man handling the outside duties that would normally require three had taken its toll on her father in the past two years. Duff McKenzie was as stubborn as his ancestors and hadn't breathed a word of complaint to Fiona while she'd been away at school

Fiona pushed the button for the tenth floor. "Dad hasn't said much, but just how bad is it?"

Britney rolled her eyes, again. "Awful. Duff's talking about selling over five hundred acres. The piece of property with the lake and hill on it. Frankly the best part of the whole ranch. I remember skinny-dipping in that lake when I was younger."

Fiona's heart ached at the news. She knew exactly which parcel they were talking about. "Why didn't he tell me it was that bad?"

Bianca laid a hand on Fiona's arm. "Your dad didn't

want you to come home until you finished your degree. He was afraid you'd abandon your education to help out."

"Damn straight I would have."

"But there wasn't much you could do. Since our mother died two years ago, medical bills have been trickling in. The drought killed cattle prices, and Duff had to sell most of the herd because he couldn't afford to feed them when the pastures dried up. That money didn't even make a dent in the bills."

"He should have told me." Fiona leaned against the elevator wall, her chest tight, and her eyes stinging.

"And you would have come home and gone to work doing what?" Bianca slipped an arm around Fiona. "Employment opportunities are practically nil for someone without a degree or trade in Temptation."

Britney picked at the polish on her fingernails. "Tell me about it."

"I've been applying for jobs, hopefully something will come up soon." She knew her salary as a special education teacher wouldn't be much, but it might help. "I can get a second job to help make ends meet. Audrey Anderson at the Ugly Stick Saloon said she'd put me to work. All I have to do is say the word."

Britney's lips twisted. "She didn't make that offer to *us*."

"Did you bother to ask?" Fiona shook her head. Sometimes she wanted to shake her sisters.

"It won't be enough or soon enough," Bianca said softly. "Dad's got a meeting with the real estate agent today. He planned it so that we would be gone while he had him over. I overheard him talking on the phone."

Fiona's stomach clenched. She had wondered why he'd been so insistent that they go visit Leslie in Dallas. Now she understood. With her off the ranch, he'd have all day to show the realtor over the property without her knowledge. Her father knew how much the ranch meant to her. It had been in the McKenzie family since their ancestors homesteaded in Texas over two hundred years ago. The McKenzie's had been one of the original Three Hundred, the group of families Steven F. Austin brought to Texas to settle.

I don't have the time for this. I should be home to stop him.

Now, Fiona didn't have the heart to stay and chat with Leslie, even though she hadn't seen her in almost a year—since she had gone with her dad last summer to attend their last session at the group grief counseling session. Her father had been in a funk since his second wife lost her battle with breast cancer. Fiona and Magnus's mother had died when she'd been thrown from a horse when Fiona and Magnus had been small.

After losing two wives in his lifetime, her father had needed the counseling. He'd been lost and depressed. Fiona had attended as many of the sessions as she could when she'd been home. At the grief counseling sessions, she'd met Leslie who'd lost her husband to pancreatic cancer. She and Fiona had become friends, keeping in touch through the Internet and telephone.

The bell rang and the elevator door swished open on the tenth floor.

A gorgeous man, dressed in a dark business suit, started to enter the elevator car, his head down as if his mind was miles ahead. When he glanced up, he stopped and took a step backward. "Pardon me."

Bianca exited, Britney following, her gaze taking in all of the man. "Oh, my."

Oh my, indeed. Even through the fog of potentially losing the ranch, Fiona couldn't help the involuntary flutter of butterflies that stirred in her belly. The man was stunning with his wavy black hair, a lock dipping down over his forehead, and piercing blue eyes that seared a path straight to her core, stirring heat she didn't know existed until then.

Fiona wondered who he was. By the fit of his tailored suit and the diamond cufflinks, he wasn't worried about losing his ranch or whatever wealthy men owned.

"Are you going down?" he said, the rich timbre of his voice humming through Fiona's insides like the reverb on stage speakers.

"What?" She blinked, struggling to gather a single coherent thought.

He smiled, making her belly turn flip-flops. "Are you getting out of the elevator or going back down?"

Britney giggled. "Come on Fi, the man is waiting for you to get out of the elevator."

As her thoughts congealed, warmth rushed into her cheeks. "Oh, sorry. I was lost in thought."

"I can tell you what thought you were lost in," Britney muttered.

Fiona hurried out of the elevator car, her heel catching on the carpet in the hallway, pitching her forward, directly into the arms of the stunning suit.

He caught her up against the wall of his muscular chest. "Steady, there."

Fiona got her feet under her and pushed against him.

At first he didn't release her and she stared up into those eyes. "I can stand on my own."

He let go and stepped back

Fiona swayed, pressing her hands to her burning cheeks. "I don't know what happened, but thank you."

"No worries." He tipped his head with a hint of a smile and entered the elevator.

Fiona's gaze remained with him as the elevator door slowly closed.

Just before she lost sight of him, the man winked.

Her heart skipped several beats, and then he was gone. Still she stood there, feeling as if something important had just happened.

"Wow, Fi." Britney giggled. "Way to impress the suit."

"Leave her alone, Brit." Bianca shot a warning look at her twin, hooked Fiona's arm and hugged it to her. "He was dreamy, wasn't he?"

Shaking her head to clear the haze, Fiona forced herself back into reality. "I don't know what you're talking about."

"Oh, come on." Britney rolled her eyes. "You practically fell all over the man."

"Yes, but only because I tripped." Fiona glared at Britney. "There's nothing funny about that."

"Tripped all over your drooling tongue." Britney laughed out loud. "You have to admit, he was very handsome."

Fiona straightened and dusted imaginary flecks off

her blouse. "And not nearly the kind of man I'm interested in."

"Why?"

"I prefer an earthy man—one who works with his hands."

Britney's giggles continued. "On you?" Tears streamed down her face.

"On the land." Fiona, with Bianca still holding her arm, stepped past Britney, pushing a startling pair of blue eyes to the back of her mind. Anger spurred Fiona forward, leaving Britney doubled over behind her.

Bianca glanced over her shoulder. "Britney, stop."

Fiona wasn't looking back to see if Britney followed or not. She wanted to get the lunch date with Leslie over and get back to the ranch where she felt more at ease. High-rise office buildings, the rush of traffic and the constant noise of the city only made her that much more uptight. The sooner she was back at home the better.

Leslie emerged from an office down the hallway. "Fiona, Britney, Bianca. So good to see you." After hugging each of them, she waved them into her office. "I was just finishing up with one of my clients. Please, come in."

Fiona entered her friend's workplace, impressed by the quiet surroundings and simple but elegant furnishings and decor. "This is lovely, Leslie. Business must be good."

"As a matter of fact, it's just beginning to take off. It's part of the reason I asked you to lunch today."

"Really?" Fiona's brows rose. "I thought we were just going to visit and catch up."

"That too. I've had lunch catered and it's in the conference room. I have something I want you to consider." She directed her comment to Fiona, her gaze bypassing Britney and Bianca.

"Us too?" Britney asked.

Leslie smiled, gently. "Not this time. Maybe in a few years."

Britney shrugged and looked around. "I smell food."

With a laugh, Leslie led them into the conference room. At one end of the solid mahogany conference table a selection of deli sandwiches, chips and muffins were tastefully arranged in front of table settings for four.

"Nice," Bianca said. "May we?"

"Please." She patted the chair at the end of the table. "Fiona, sit here."

"What's this all about?" Not sure about the way Leslie was acting, she slid into the seat, her appetite on hold until Leslie unveiled whatever she'd invited her there to demonstrate.

"Sit back, relax and watch the six-minute video. I'll answer your questions when it's over." Leslie sat beside her and plucked a sandwich off the tray. "Don't worry. I'm not going to sell you something or ask you to come to work for me in the city. I know you prefer the country. Just keep an open mind." She set her sandwich on the plate in front of her and lifted a remote control, clicked a button and the lights dimmed in the room.

"Fancy," Britney said between bites of her sandwich.

With another click, a couple appeared on the screen, standing on a beach at sunset, kissing.

The image reminded Fiona of her own lack of a love

life. Six minutes later, she realized that was exactly what it was supposed to do.

"What exactly do you want me to do with this online dating system?" Fiona asked.

Leslie grinned. "I want you to consider being one of my hand-selected entrants into the system."

Fiona hadn't taken a single bite out of a sandwich. "You want me to date someone from your system?"

She nodded. "That's right. As I said in the video, I hand-select all my clients. They have to be decent, relatively attractive women who aren't afraid of hard work and who would make good partners in relationships. I immediately thought of you."

"I just graduated college. I don't even have a paying job yet."

"Hey, what about us?" Britney tapped her napkin to her lips. "Where do I sign?"

"Sorry, you two," Leslie winked. "I like my clients to be a little older."

Britney pouted. "I'll be twenty-one in nine months."

Bianca whispered, "Shh. Let her finish."

Leslie laid a hand on Fiona's arm, a gentle smile on her face. "How long has it been since you had a decent date?"

Fiona stood, pushing her chair back with enough force the wheels carried it back three feet before it stopped. "I don't know. It doesn't matter."

"From what you've told me, you've been burning the candle at both ends to work and go to school at the same time. You could use a break."

"I can't take a break. I have responsibilities." Fiona paced the length of the long conference table and back.

"Dad needs help on the ranch. I have to find a job. Britney and Bianca have State Boards coming up."

Bianca's brows furrowed. "Fiona, you're pushing too hard. You deserve a little fun."

Fiona sank into the chair and stared across at Leslie. "I can't. I haven't had time for dating because I don't have time for a relationship. Between teaching—when I land a teaching job—ranching and any other paying work I can get, I won't have a lot of spare time. Men who go on a site like this are looking for commitment. Something more than a once-a-month kind of thing."

"My system isn't the same as the others. And you need to put yourself first or you'll waste your youth." Leslie placed her hand over Fiona's. "I think you're wonderful, sweetie. I know there's someone out there perfect for you. At least think about it." She pressed a business card into her hand. "If you'd prefer to enter your information in private, you can log onto the system from home."

Fiona laid the card on the table, shaking her head. "I'm not interested, Leslie. I hope your business does great, but I can't do this right now."

"Okay, but promise me you'll at least think about it." Leslie slipped the card in Fiona's purse. "No pressure."

"Okay." Fiona stood. "Britney, Bianca, I really need to get back to the ranch before Dad decides to do something really stupid."

"But I didn't get my desert," Britney brushed the breadcrumbs from her fingertips, having polished off one of the sandwiches.

Bianca wrapped her sandwich in a napkin, giving Leslie a weak smile. "I guess we're leaving."

Leslie stood, her disappointment obvious in the slump of her shoulders. She held the plate of muffins out to Britney and Bianca. "Take some with you. Please."

Britney chose a blueberry muffin and wrapped it in a napkin.

Bianca selected a lemon poppy seed muffin to take with her sandwich. "Thank you for lunch."

"It was great to see you again," Britney added.

"You two have matured a lot since the last time I saw you." Leslie tipped her head. "Maybe a couple more years and I'll invite you to participate."

"Count me in. I think it's a great idea," Britney said.

"Good luck, Leslie," Bianca hugged Leslie.

Last to leave, Fiona paused. "I'm sorry, but you understand, don't you?"

Leslie embraced her. "I do, more than you can know. But you aren't responsible for everyone. You need a life of your own."

Her gaze following her stepsisters, Fiona sighed. "If I don't look out for them, who will?"

"Everything has a way of working out." Leslie kissed her cheek. "Go home, Fiona. Even if you don't use the system, at least get out there. You don't want to miss out on a loving relationship, like I had."

Fiona's lips twisted into a wry grin. "I'm not sure you're a good example."

"That's where you're wrong." Leslie's gaze drifted toward the hallway as if seeing the man she'd lost. "My husband died too young, but I wouldn't trade any of those memories for all the world's riches."

"Better to have loved and lost—" Fiona started.

"—than never to have loved at all," Leslie finished. "Promise me you'll think about it."

Bianca and Britney ducked their heads back into the office. "She will," they said in unison.

"Fiona?" Leslie prompted. "Promise?"

Fiona laughed, the warmth of Leslie's hug and the depth of her emotions seeping into her. If she didn't have so many worries on her plate...

"I promise."

CHAPTER 3

"Thanks again for loaning me your truck." Gage hit the speaker button on his cell phone and set it in the cup holder. He'd had his chauffeur drop him at the Jacobs' ranch where Frank met him with his truck.

"Emma's excited that you're first date is with Fiona McKenzie," Frank's voice filled the cab of the truck.

"I'm still not completely sold on this idea. At the very least, I hope it beats the options I have in Dallas."

"From all Emma's said about Fiona, you'll be okay."

"I have no idea what to expect."

"Didn't you read her profile?"

"No. I didn't have time. I put my faith in Leslie and her software." He tapped his fingers on the steering wheel. "Speaking of Emma, where is she? I could use some advice on what to say and where to take her. I've never been to Temptation."

"There's not much in the town. PJ's Diner and the local truck stop are about the only places you can get a decent meal."

"And you come here by choice?" Gage said, thinking of the plethora of fine dining available in Dallas and his driver to get him there. Although, he had to admit, it felt good to get out on the open road outside the big city traffic, riding high in a truck.

Frank laughed. "I love it here. But then I've always enjoyed the ranch life."

"I just hope she has all of her teeth." He turned off the road at the gate with the faded sign indicating Rafter M Ranch.

"At least you don't have to run the gauntlet of four brothers. From what Emma said, Fiona only has one brother and he works in Hole in the Wall."

"There's really a town called Hole in the Wall?" Gage almost turned the truck around and drove back to the Jacob's ranch where his chauffeur was settling in to watch the football game on television with the Jacobs brothers, Frank and Emma. He envied them. Instead of having a beer and relaxing, he was putting himself out there for a stranger the BODS system churned up for him. What if they had nothing in common? Gage cringed, imaging endless minutes of awkward silence. "Are you sure Leslie hand-picked the applicants?"

"Don't worry. One date is all you have to give this woman. If it doesn't work out, Leslie will have BODS find you another."

"You're not making me feel any better here." The connection crackled. "I'm losing you. See you later."

"Have fun."

Having come from meetings and doing work the entire way in the back of the limousine, he'd had little time to study the dossier his bodyguard Hal had prepared on Fiona McKenzie. He paused just inside the gate and flipped through the pages.

Reddish brown hair, green eyes, five feet seven inches—typical information he could get from a driver's license. Then he noticed her birth date. "Hell, she's only twenty-four." Nine years younger than he was. What would he have in common with someone that young? She was barely out of school. He looked again at the date on her undergraduate degree, blinked and looked again. Last month. A bachelor's degree in education.

"I don't need this. She's too young. We'll have nothing in common and I'm wasting my time."

He shifted the truck into reverse with all intentions of turning around and getting the hell of there. Then the thought of some poor woman waiting for her date that never showed pricked his conscience. As busy as he was, he couldn't stand her up. The least he owed her was to make a showing, tell her he'd made a mistake and then he could leave with a clear conscience.

Shifting the truck back into drive, he drove down the rutted gravel road, winding through shady oak trees. When he thought he'd gone a pretty long way and was beginning to wonder if he'd turned onto the wrong road, the trees thinned and opened into a clearing at the center of which was an old colonial-style home with wide porches and tall windows.

He'd hoped the woman he was to meet was waiting on the porch so that he could get this over with and get back on the road to Dallas.

But no. The porch was empty and the only greeting he got was from a three-legged black lab, limping down the steps.

The words, *big mistake*, echoed through his mind as he climbed down from the pickup.

"I'M HEADED out to the northern section." Fiona's father leaned through the stall door where she worked. "I noticed a section of fence down back there."

Fiona paused from raking the old hay and horse manure into a pile in Lightning's stall and glanced up. "Want me to go with you?"

"No, I'll be fine. There's plenty of work to do around here." In the years she'd been away for her last semesters of college, the lines had been etched even deeper into her father's leathery skin.

"Dad, you're not sneaking another realtor out there are you?"

He removed his hat and slapped it against his thigh. "You weren't supposed to know about that."

She grinned. "Yeah, but you can't keep secrets in this house."

"Not with those two busybodies," her father groused. "Should have kicked them out after high school."

"Yeah, right, Dad. You love Bianca and Britney like your own." Which was true. When he'd brought their mother home as his wife, they'd been three years old. They'd wrapped all the McKenzies around their little pinkies within the first week.

"Yeah, but they shouldn't have told you."

"Dad." Fiona leaned her rake against the wall and crossed to her dad. "I'm home now. We can work this out. You don't have to sell that property."

"Baby, you don't know how bad it is." He raked a

hand through his graying hair. "I can't keep pushing off paying the bills. The doctors and nurses who were with Desiree to the end deserve to be paid."

"I know, but this land has been in the McKenzie family since they came over from Scotland. We can't sell it."

"Times change. Small ranchers and farmers can't compete with the conglomerations. This place has been losing money for a while."

"Before you sell it, let me look at the books."

He shrugged. "I've looked a hundred times. It's not good. Sometimes, you gotta know when to let go."

Problem was, she didn't want to let go. "This is McKenzie land."

"No one knows that more than you, me and Magnus." Her father snorted. "And he has to work as a mechanic. I couldn't pay him to ranch."

Fiona's eyes stung and her heart squeezed hard in her chest. "There has to be something we can do."

"Selling is all I know. I'm too old to find another job. And I won't have you working to keep this place afloat. I won't take money you make from your job to fund this ranch."

"I don't have a job yet. But if I want to spend my money on this place, I will."

"It will be like sticking your finger in a broken dam. The medical bills sealed this ranch's fate. Besides, my heart isn't in it anymore. Losing your mother was bad."

"Oh, Dad." She hugged her father. "I loved them too. Granted, at first, I didn't *want* to love Desiree, but she never tried to replace mom and she made you happy. I couldn't have asked for more from her, unless it was more years spent with you."

Her father's eyes misted and he scrubbed a hand down his face. "The point is, this family has suffered enough. I won't have you add Magnus trying to keep the ranch afloat when it's only a matter of time before the bank forecloses."

Fiona's heart ached. "I don't want to lose our home."

"Baby," her father smiled across at her. "It's just a place." He kissed the top of her head. "People are what matter."

"I know." She hugged him again and stepped away before she cried. "It's getting close to dinnertime— don't be out after dark. I don't want to have to come looking for you." She winked.

"Yes, ma'am." He plunked his hat on his head, climbed on a four-wheeler loaded with fencing equipment and drove off across the pasture.

Fiona went back to work on the stall, brushing tears from her cheeks. This was the only home she'd ever known. She'd be damned if she lost one acre of it without putting up a fight.

Minutes later, Britney burst through the barn door. "Fiona, Bianca needs you in the house, right now."

Fiona looked up from mucking a horse stall. "Now?"

"Now!" Britney looked back over her shoulder. "Hurry." Then she ran out the door.

Seeing the panic on the unflappable Britney's face, Fiona leaned the pitchfork against the wall and ran after Britney. "What's wrong?"

Her stepsister never answered or slowed, staying way ahead of Fiona as she ran in her cowboy boots all the way up to the back of the house. Britney disappeared inside.

When Fiona stepped through the back door, she sniffed, didn't smell smoke, and muttered, "Where's the fire?" Then louder, she called out, "Bianca?"

"In the bathroom," she called out. "Hurry."

Britney was nowhere to be seen.

Fiona ran through the house, cursing as she left behind a trail of horse manure from her cowboy boots. She found Bianca in the bathroom she shared with the other two girls, standing next to the tub. "Bianca, what's wrong?" When she entered the bathroom, the door slammed shut behind her. Fiona squealed and spun toward Britney who blocked the door and held up her hands.

"Don't be mad," Britney started.

"She made me do it," Bianca insisted.

"For your own good," Britney insisted.

Fiona stared from one girl to the other. "Be mad about what?" She lifted Bianca's hands and ran her gaze over her. No blood. "Are you okay?"

The girl's hands shook in hers. "I am *now*, but I won't be after we tell you what we did."

Fiona's eyes narrowed. "Will someone tell me what's going on?"

"We entered your name in BODS, and your date is getting out of his truck as we speak," Britney said all in a rush.

"You did what?" Pressure rose in her head and threatened to explode.

Bianca moved the shower curtain aside. "He's here.

You have to shower. We'll stall him." She pinched her nose closed. "Please, you really smell."

"I'm not done in the barn, and I'm not going out with someone *you two* set me up with." She turned to leave, but Britney blocked the door.

"Please. He's come all the way from Dallas. You can't send him away without at least saying something to him."

"I'm not going to say something to him, you two are. Now move, so I can finish cleaning out the stall."

"We'll do it," Bianca burst in. "Britney and I'll finish all the chores in the barn."

Fiona crossed her arms over her chest. "You two barely know where the barn is."

"We did the chores all the time you were gone."

"Without Dad telling you a hundred times?"

The twins had the decency to blush.

Britney confessed, "Well, he did remind us a few times."

Bianca elbowed her sister. "Every day."

"Still, even if you did my chores, I'm not going out with the guy. I have no desire to sit across the table from someone I've never met. He probably doesn't know where a steak comes from or couldn't tell one end of a horse from another. I don't have time to deal with someone like that."

"Then don't go out," Bianca said, her face brightening. "Offer to take him riding. If he doesn't want to, we'll show him to the door. If he does, you can see how committed he is to getting to know you, and how comfortable he is in the outdoors. You can make it a picnic. Britney and I'll make sandwiches for you. Won't we, Britney?"

Britney's brows dipped. "Hey, first you volunteer us to muck stalls, now we're making sandwiches?"

The usually soft-spoken Bianca glared at her twin. "*You* got us into this, *you* can help."

"*You* agreed it was a good idea for Fi to date."

A loud knock on the outside of the house echoed all the way into the bathroom.

Fiona jumped, her heart beating faster than she cared to admit. "Whatever you two do, do it now. Someone's knocking at the door."

"What should we tell him?" Bianca gripped Fiona's arm. "Please don't make us tell him to go away without at least saying hello to him."

Fiona could think of a hundred other things she'd rather do, including getting a root canal, than to go on a blind date she didn't even agree to in the first place. But she'd never been able to say no to Bianca once she got that pleading look on her face. "Fine, I'll meet him. But that's all I'm committing to. As for the picnic, it's getting too late to ride, the sun's setting."

"What better time to ride?" Britney sighed. "Riding off into the sunset with your handsome stranger. You can't get more romantic than that."

Closing her eyes, Fiona drew on all her patience before responding. "He's not my handsome stranger, and I'm not getting all romantic with a man I've never met. He's probably bald, missing a few teeth and chews tobacco."

"Oh, Fi, you have that all wrong," Bianca said.

Britney practically bounced. "We looked at his profile."

Bianca finished with, "He's incredibly handsome."

"And he has all his hair," Britney concluded.

"He probably fudged the system with someone else's photograph." Not that Fiona cared. She didn't have time to date when the ranch was in jeopardy.

"Leslie assured us the photo was real," Britney grabbed her hands. "He's that handsome."

Bianca nodded. "Leslie knows him personally."

Fiona raised her hand, a twinge of guilt pinching her conscience. Leslie was her friend, and she hated to disappoint her, especially when she was trying so hard to launch her new business. Still... "I don't care. I'll meet him. That's all. You two get to apologize for deceiving him and then send him on his way."

Britney frowned. "But—"

Bianca pulled her sister back. "That's all we ask. Oh, and that you get a shower first."

"You really smell." Britney waved a hand in front of her nose.

"All I have to do is show up clean and meet the guy." A smile teased Fiona's lips. "And you two will muck the stalls?"

"We will." Britney stuck out her hand.

Fiona shook it and Bianca cranked the handle on the shower.

"Go stall the man while I jump in the shower. And no, I'm not drying my hair just for him, or wearing makeup."

"At least wear a little lipstick." Britney urged.

"No makeup." She didn't plan on the date going past a polite hello. No use giving the man false hope.

The twins ducked out of the bathroom as another knock sounded on the front door.

She'd planned on spending the evening pouring over the ranch accounts. Based on what her father had said about the financial condition of the land, she'd be better off finding a summer job right away. Her resume was out to the schools in the tri-county area, but she needed something now. If she wasn't mistaken, she'd seen a posting for a waitress job at the Ugly Stick Saloon. Audrey had always said she had a job whenever she needed it. She'd heard from Charli Sutton that the tips were good and Audrey Anderson was a sweetheart to work for.

Fiona stripped out of her clothes and jumped into the shower. She needed to smell good anyway. Especially if she was job hunting. As she washed the smell of the barnyard off her body, she whistled, happy with herself for tricking her stepsisters into doing the chores and making her dinner.

And they'd have to break it to the *date* that she wasn't the one who'd set it up. It was a win-win situation all around.

CHAPTER 4

AFTER TWO KNOCKS, Gage turned to leave and almost tripped over the three-legged dog. The animal wagged his tail, his entire body wagging with it. Gage leaned down and scratched the dog behind the ears. "Seems you're the only one happy to see me."

As he straightened, he didn't know whether to be annoyed or relieved. On the one hand, he wouldn't be forced to spend the next two to three hours making inane conversation with a stranger when he could be back in his office checking the status of the projects he had going.

Though Leslie had assured him this Fiona McKenzie was a very attractive woman with a college degree, he had only to look around the ranch house and surroundings to realize the degree hadn't bought her much thus far. The house needed the peeling paint scraped off and a couple of new coats to protect what appeared to be one-hundred-year-old wood siding.

He climbed down from the porch, one of the steps

giving more than the others as though the wood beneath had rotted and needed replacing. Gage had started his business remodeling homes while going to college on loans and scholarships at Texas A&M University. He knew when a house had good bones, even when the paint was peeling and the roof needed replacing. His gift had been the power to see the potential in a piece of property. After he'd completed his degree in architecture, he'd interned with one of the major architectural firms in Dallas, rising quickly as one of the most talented architects.

He'd lucked into a piece of property in downtown Dallas, an old warehouse others had considered worthy only of demolishing. He'd purchased the property, hawking everything he owned and going into more debt than he ever imagined. It had been a gamble and one he'd bet his life on.

That project had been a huge risk, but had proven to be only the beginning of his rise to prominence. He'd taken that run-down property and turned it into loft apartments for the very wealthy. It became *the* place to live in downtown Dallas. His burgeoning business exploded, and he had more work than he could get to. Within a couple years, he was building exquisitely designed high-rises. Now he had more money than he knew what to do with.

His life was hectic and it wasn't unusual for him to work eighty or ninety hours a week. Often he'd find himself staring out the window of his office at the Dallas skyline, wondering if he'd given up too much. Perhaps, proposing to Lacy had been an insane attempt to reclaim what he'd lost in his rise to the top of his field. When he'd purchased the engagement ring, he'd considered buying a tract of land and returning to his country roots. After Lacy threw his proposal back in his face, Gage immersed himself in his work, pushing aside his personal life, more attracted to the next challenge than to the women he met in Dallas.

As he glanced out across the rolling hills of sweet-scented hay, something tugged at his insides. His friends had ranches and swore by the peace and tranquility of being surrounded by acres and acres of nothing but grass, trees and animals.

For the first time in a long time, Gage could understand what they saw in it. If he wasn't so tied up trying to come to an accord with the owner of particularly choice piece of property in downtown Dallas, he might again consider a home in the country.

The sun slid toward the horizon. As the bright orange orb sank lower, it tinged the puffy white clouds purple and mauve, ringing them in a brilliant gilded outline. Yeah, he could see how a man could fall in love with the country setting. But the sun setting over the Dallas skyline could be just as entrancing.

He shrugged and started for the truck, relieved that he could head back to Dallas while there was still a little light left in the sky.

"Mr. Tate!" a female voice called out.

Gage swallowed a groan and considered bolting for the truck, pretending that he hadn't heard the shout.

"Please, Mr. Tate, wait," a similar voice, only different called out and seemed to be closer.

Caught before he could make good his escape, Gage turned to face two young women, both blond and nothing like the photo he'd glanced at in the dossier Leslie had provided. And they were vaguely familiar. His brows pulled together. He'd only signed up for a date with one woman not carbon-copied blondes.

"Thank goodness, you're still here," the woman nearest him said. "Please, won't you come inside and wait? My sister is running a little behind." She hurried forward and hooked his arm.

"Yes, please. Come inside." The woman still standing on the steps waved a hand toward the door. "I just made a pitcher of sweet tea, if you'd care for some."

"No thank you," he said, trying to come up with a good reason to leave and falling short. Although ruthless in business, he couldn't be out-and-out rude to the women leading…no… dragging him into the house. What had he been thinking when he'd agreed to Leslie's experiment in matchmaking? All he needed was a date for the charity ball. This house…these women…had commitment written all over them and he was letting them drag him into their web. Their sister must be pretty desperate to assign these two to do her dirty work.

"Please, won't you have a seat?" The one holding his arm asked, pointing to a faded brown couch in the spacious living room.

With both women blocking his escape, he had no other choice but take the seat. "If your sister is too busy to go out, we can call this whole thing off."

"No!" both women exclaimed at once.

In a calmer voice, the one beside him extended her hand. "I'm Bianca."

"Ga—Austin Tate." Gage stumbled over his name, shook the hand and let go.

Bianca pointed to the other woman. "Austin, this is my sister, Britney."

Britney held out her hand. "We're Fiona's stepsisters."

That would explain the difference in hair color. "Nice to meet you."

"Would you like that tea, now?" Bianca asked.

What he really wanted was to get the hell out of there, head back to his own vehicle where he could pour himself a double whiskey on the rocks and work the kinks out of the project that had fallen three weeks behind while his driver took him back to Dallas. This was a huge mistake. "No thank you."

"I'll just go check on Fi." Bianca slipped out of the room, leaving Britney there.

She smiled. "Aren't you the man we ran into in the elevator the day we visited Leslie?"

Ah, that feeling he'd seen these women before had been justified as he recalled the incident in the elevator. "Yes. You were with someone else." The other woman in the elevator had captured his attention more than the blondes. Her dark eyes had seemed to burn right through him, and her body up against his had ignited something he hadn't felt in a very long time.

Passion. His pulse kicked up a notch and he found himself leaning forward. When he realized what he was doing, he immediately sat back, telling himself the woman in the elevator would be like all the rest. Interesting at first, but easily swayed by the monetary potential of dating a very wealthy man.

"You're even better looking than the photo on BODS," Britney said.

Gage forced a smile, the urge to get out of the house back in full force. With only one woman standing in his way now, he could easily slide by and be on his way.

Britney leaned nearer. "And you smell good too. What is it? Borneo? Clive Christian?" She lifted her nose and moved even closer until she almost fell into his lap. "It smells expensive."

"Nothing that fancy. Just soap." Gage rose and moved away. "Really, I should be going."

Britney's eyes widened. "You can't go without first meeting Fiona."

"She doesn't seem to be in a hurry to meet with me."

"Only because she didn't know about you until—"

"Britney!" Bianca entered the room, glaring at her twin. "Fiona will be out momentarily. I'm sure you'll be glad you waited."

Gage wasn't so certain. The longer he waited the more convinced he became that the whole online match program wasn't the way to go. He'd be better off hiring an escort. Someone he could pay to be his date, no strings attached.

Britney whispered to Bianca, "He's the man from the elevator."

Bianca's eyes widened and her gaze raked him from tip to toe, her lips spreading into a smile. "Oh my God, he is."

The prickly feeling a deer must get when being hunted washed over Gage. He shook it off and stood. "Look, if your sister isn't interested in going out, no need to bother her."

"Where are you going?" Bianca stepped in front of him.

"I wasn't completely sold on using an online dating system and by all appearances, neither was your sister. Please relate my sincere apologies to her."

"You can do it yourself." Another feminine voice sounded behind Bianca. "And frankly, that suits me just fine."

Gage glanced past the blonde to the woman standing in the hallway, pulling the strap of her purse over her shoulder. She wore a white tank top with a red, white and blue beer logo on the front and frayed shorts that barely covered her ass. Wet hair was combed smooth away from her forehead and fell down her back in long damp curls. Her curves accentuated the tank top and the short shorts. The red, white and blue cowboy boots only added to the overall package, quite a transformation from the well-dressed woman who'd fallen into his arms getting off the elevator.

Though she was sexy as hell in it, the outfit would better fit a teenager or a waitress at Hooters. It wasn't what Gage considered an outfit suitable for a blind date.

The woman in front of him with the clean, girl-next-door face and legs from her chin to her toes, appeared to be on her way to shoot an advertisement for the beer company emblazoned across the shirt stretched over her ample chest.

With her make-up-free face, damp hair and the scent of honeysuckle shampoo wafting his way, she set off everything raw and sexual in Gage.

A flash of recognition widened her eyes. Just as quickly as it came, a curtain seemed to drop over her face and she stepped around her sisters. "Hi, I'm Fiona. I'm sorry you drove all the way down here from Dallas, but sadly you were duped. And I have other plans." She cocked her dark brows. "And based on your blank expression, I take it my sisters haven't told you that this was their idea."

His pulse zipped through his veins, thrumming to an internal primitive beat. He had to focus hard to comprehend her words when his brain cells had dived south. "Pardon me if I'm not clued in." Gage took her hand in his and an electric shock ran up his arm and spread throughout his body. His groin tightened and his fingers curled around hers. "Fiona."

For a very brief moment, Fiona's irises flared, but then her jaw tightened. "Well, I'll leave Britney and Bianca to explain. I'm sorry they led you on a wild goose chase. Perhaps you can take one of them out on a date instead. Nice to meet you." She had to tug her hand to get it out of his grip.

"You didn't agree to the match on Leslie's system?" Gage asked.

Fiona gave him a bright smile. "That would be correct. I didn't, and I really have to leave. Bianca can explain."

Bianca, her cheeks flushing a bright pink, gave her stepsister a pleading look. "Fiona, please."

The beautiful brunette turned to the blondes. "You two set this up, I'm sure you can figure it out."

Gage frowned. He didn't like being the object of anyone having to "figure him out." He could get a date anytime he wanted. But the way Fiona put it made him sound like he was a pathetic loser who'd had to resort to an online dating system to get a date. Before he could speak up, Fiona executed an about face and left the room.

"Fiona!" her sisters called after her.

"Handle it," she said without slowing. The click of boots on the porch heralded her departure, followed by the rev of a truck engine. She'd left.

Stunned, Gage stared out the window at the departing truck. This situation was new to him. He'd never been stood up for a date. Irritation and something else burned through him—that same something he'd felt when Fiona fell into him coming off the elevator in Dallas.

Britney and Bianca turned sheepish faces toward Gage.

Bianca was first to speak. "I'm sorry. This is all our fault."

Gage leveled his most fierce glare at the two young women. "You two set her up for this date?"

They nodded simultaneously.

"Where is she heading?" he demanded before he even thought about the question. Why he asked, he couldn't fathom. The woman obviously was not interested in him.

Britney shrugged.

Bianca's brow furrowed. "Based on the way she was dressed, she was headed for the rodeo, which isn't until late in the summer, or she's going to the Ugly Stick Saloon."

Gage nodded. "Ladies, thank you for your time." He started to step around them, but Britney blocked him yet again. He was beginning to feel caged.

"You don't want to take one of us out, do you?" Britney smiled, her eyes wide, hopeful.

"No, thank you," he said. "Though you both are very pretty, I like to date women who are closer to my age." Gage arched his brows. "Now, if you don't mind, I'd like to leave."

Bianca hooked Britney's arm and yanked her out of the way. "Let the man go. We've taken up enough of his time." She held out her hand. "We're sorry we wasted your time. You might find women closer to your age at the Ugly Stick. It's only ten minutes down the road at the crossroads between Temptation and Hole in the Wall."

He wanted to say he wasn't that desperate, but settled for, "Thank you, but I think I'll head back to Dallas." Gage strode for the door while the path was clear.

"It's a long way to Dallas, especially if you're thirsty," Bianca added, following him out the door and onto the porch.

"I'm sure I'll be fine." He flashed a smile at the two women. "Thank you for the interesting afternoon." Without waiting for their response, he climbed into the truck, turned around in the gravel drive and hurried away thanking his lucky stars he'd escaped.

Fiona McKenzie. The name suited her red hair and fierce determination.

His hand still tingled where he'd touched hers.

Damn.

Gage turned toward the Jacob's ranch where his driver would be happy to take him home and get an early night off. When he pulled up to the ranch house, all four Jacobs brothers, Emma and Frank stepped out on the porch, every one of them sporting a frown as Gage climbed down from the truck.

"What happened?" Emma asked, first to break the silence. "Wasn't she there?"

Gage nodded. "She was."

Emma's eyes rounded. "She turned you down? How was that even possible?" She ran a glance over him. "I mean look at you."

Cooper's frown deepened and he slipped a possessive arm around Emma's waist. "Should I be jealous?"

Emma leaned into Coop. "No. But damn, Gage is almost as good looking as you."

Raking a hand through his hair, Gage's lips twisted in a wry grin. "Apparently her stepsisters set up the date without her knowledge. She'd made other plans for the evening."

"What other plans would be better than going out with Texas's most eligible bachelor?" Brand Jacobs said.

Gage stared off into the distance, his thoughts on the way Fiona had filled out the tank top and frayed shorts. Not one single Dallas debutante would be caught dead wearing an outfit like that in public. But damned if Fiona didn't look good enough to give him a painful boner. Just the thought of her in those shorts made him hard all over again. "Her stepsisters said something about the Ugly Stick Saloon."

Emma's lips twitched upward on the corners. She turned to Cooper. "You know what that means, right?"

Coop scowled. "That I'm supposed to read your mind?"

She grabbed his hand. "No. It means we're going out tonight."

"We are?" He pulled her into his arms. "I can think of better things to do than to spend my evening packed into a crowded bar when I'd rather be alone with you."

"Hey." Ace Jacobs, Emma's oldest brother, back-handed Coop in the gut. "Spare us. She is our sister and you're making me want to slug you."

Coop cinched his arms around Emma's waist and lifted her off her feet, covering her mouth with his in a loud, exuberant kiss. When he set her down, he grinned. "Get your dancing boots on, baby, we're going to the Ugly Stick tonight."

The Jacobs men all hooted and slapped their hats against their thighs.

Gage pushed away from the post he'd been leaning against. "I hope you enjoy it. I'm headed back to Dallas."

"Like hell you are." Emma left Coop's side and grabbed his arm to keep him from leaving. "You're coming with us. If the lady won't come to you, you have to go to her."

"I did and she wasn't interested." Gage shrugged.

"She was hoodwinked." Emma refused to let go of Gage's arm. "You have to meet her on her own terms."

"I really need to get back to Dallas. I have a business to run, and I'm perfectly capable of getting a date without going through an online dating service."

Emma let go of his arm and planted her fists on her hips. "Then why did you agree to the date match in the first place?"

"I can tell you why." Coop grinned. "His image consultant insisted he needed an image boost."

Emma nodded. "And that's the reason for hosting the charity ball instead of just being a silent contributor this year?"

Gage gave Coop a killer glare then nodded. "Much as I hate big social events, they are a necessary evil. The charity ball is a huge fundraiser for abused children."

"And he needs this event to make him look less of a ruthless bastard." Coop draped an arm over Gage's shoulder. "Is that right?"

Gage stiffened. "I wouldn't put it that bluntly, but yes."

"Why don't you go stag to the ball?" Emma asked.

"I told someone I already had a date."

Emma's brows hiked. "So?"

"So, if I show up without a date, she'll think I lied."

"Well, you did, didn't you?" Emma gave him a pointed stare.

"I had to, or I would have been railroaded into taking her."

"So go to the ball and tell the woman your date got sick at the last minute," Emma offered.

Gage had thought of that. "If I did that, this woman would cling to me the entire evening." He shivered. "No." He sighed, hating that he was going to the event in the first place. But he'd hired Haddie Madison to help him improve his image. "She suggested I choose someone whose record is as clean as a whistle." He didn't add that Haddie had suggested he treat his date with respect, not date and dump her like all his women.

"Why not take one of the Dallas debutantes? What were their names? Priscilla and Marilyn?" Coop suggested.

Gage shook his head. "Priscilla Langley is definitely off limits. I want to buy property from her father. Dating her would only complicate the acquisition. Marilyn is her friend, and if that isn't bad enough, Marilyn's mother would have all of Dallas and half the country convinced we were getting married if I showed up to the ball with either of them."

"So?" Coop said.

"When we broke up my reputation would be back in the crapper again along with the deal I've been working on for the past six months."

"Langley Place in downtown Dallas," Coop added.

Gage nodded. "Haddie, my image consultant, spoke with William Langley's executive assistant. He shared that the only thing holding Langley back from selling to me is that he thinks I'm too young and too brash."

"You are young." Emma's pretty brows puckered. "But what does he mean about brash?"

Cooper laughed out loud. "That translates to a man who can't settle on one woman."

"Why is that brash?" she asked. "He just hasn't met the right one."

"Langley thinks Gage is too full of himself, and he's playing with the affections of the women he's gone out with."

Gage pressed his fingers to the bridge of his nose. "You don't have to discuss me as if I'm not here."

"Mr. Langley thinks Gage doesn't respect women, and he's holding out selling the property to him even though Gage has offered him more than what he's asking." Coop crossed his arms over his chest. "Isn't that right?"

"I offered him more than a fair price. The man's a stubborn fool."

Cooper's brows rose. "Do you know that Langley, for all his money and holdings, was married to his first and only wife for fifty-five years before she passed away?"

"Their relationship was an anomaly. Over forty percent of all marriages end in divorce. Forty percent." Gage snorted. "Why bother getting married in the first place?"

Emma's brows furrowed. "You make it sound like the noose of a hangman? Marriage is a commitment to love one person the rest of your life."

"It's overrated and outdated."

Emma smacked the back of her hand against Coop's chest. "He's *your* friend. Should I be worried you feel the same way?"

Coop raised his hands. "Don't get me into this fight. If the man doesn't believe in marriage, that's his business."

Emma glared at Coop and then faced Gage. "Gage, you're taking advantage of the women you date, leading them to believe they might actually have a chance with you."

Gage shook his head. "I usually make it abundantly clear that I'm only going out to dinner and a show. If we have sex afterward, I let them know up front there are no guarantees that I'll call them again. And I tell them this before we commit to the act."

Emma snorted. "How noble. I see why Langley doesn't trust you."

Gage bristled. "When I make a promise, I follow through."

"So you avoid making any promises to the women you date."

Now Emma was getting it. Gage's lips lifted in a hint of a smile. "Precisely."

Her eyes narrowed and her lips pressed into a tight line. "Then by all means, head back to Dallas. I'd hate for you to hurt one of our local gals in your game of heartless dating." She glanced up at Coop. "Still wanna go to the Ugly Stick? I could use a little fun after all the hot air around here. And I'll bet Fiona could use some better company."

Coop nuzzled her neck. "Ready when you are."

The sweet little cowgirl Coop had fallen head over heels for scowled at Gage. "Cooper, I'm not so sure I like your friend."

A hard knot twisted in Gage's gut. He'd liked Emma the first time he'd met her. From outward appearances, she loved Coop unconditionally, and he was crazy about her. They seemed to light up in each other's company.

Gage wondered what that felt like and almost envied them their open displays of affection. But he knew it for what it was worth. Once the lust wore off, they'd get tired of each other quickly and what they thought was love would fade.

Like whatever bond had been between Gage's mother and father.

Why invest a lot of emotion in someone you'd get bored with, or who would be bored with you? Emotion made people weak. He wouldn't be where he was today if he'd allowed more than a mild attraction. Hell, he simply couldn't afford the time or emotional commitment a relationship involved. Gage knew his limitations and he made it an unwritten rule never to date a woman more than two times. Anything past two and she started demanding more of him, expecting him to call or to drop by.

Emma's brother, Dillon leaped down from the porch. "I didn't know Fiona McKenzie was back in town. Seems I ran into her a couple years ago at the Ugly Stick. Damned fine-looking woman then. Wonder if she's still as pretty." He clamped his cowboy hat on his head. "It's been a busy week, I'm due a little fun, maybe some two-steppin'."

Emma's brother, Colton winked at Gage. "Guess I'll go along and show you how it's done. How old is little Fiona?"

"Twenty-three or four, I think." Dillon scowled at his brother. "Too young for you, old man."

Colton hooked his belt loops with his thumbs and rocked back on his heels. "Hey, I'm only thirty."

"And getting long in the tooth." Dillon pulled his keys from his pocket. "Now that it's dark outside, the place should be hoppin'."

Gage knew he should leave, but Dillon and Colton's talk of seeing Fiona at the Ugly Stick gave Gage a renewed interest in the woman. Not to mention the way his fingers still tingled from when he'd touched her.

So, she'd stood him up. It really hadn't been her fault. Her sisters had put her name in the system.

And he still needed a date to the charity ball. The

thought of going with Priscilla or Marilyn made him want to grind his teeth to nubs. One way or another he'd find a date, even if he had to choose someone from a bar in the country.

"Fine. I'll go with you," Gage said.

Colton and Dillon squared off with Gage, staring him down.

"Fiona looks good as long as someone else is interested in her? Is that it?" Dillon asked.

"I've come this far from Dallas, I might as well get something out of the trip. A beer and some country music might get me in the mood for the long drive back."

"Yeah, right." Colton glanced around at his brothers. "Who's riding with me?"

Dillon jiggled his keys. "I'm taking my own. If I get lucky, I don't want you horning in on my catch." He winked at Gage. "Might even be Fiona. As far as I'm concerned, she's fair game."

"You'll have to beat me to her." Colton took off at a lope, headed for his truck.

"Who wants to ride with us?" Coop gathered Emma's hand.

Ace shrugged. "I will. I imagine you two won't stay long, and I'm not into closing the bar tonight. I'm riding fences tomorrow. Had a couple of trees fall and a bull pushed a hole in another. I'll be stringing wire and pounding T-posts all day."

"I'll ride with Colton." Brand hurried after his brother.

Ace tipped his head toward Gage. "How about it,

Gage? Are you taking your own hired car or will you ride with one of us?"

He glanced at the sleek black car. In Dallas, it blended in. In the wilds of Texas, it stuck out like a piece of gaudy jewelry on a pig. He'd had the driver bring him to Temptation to give him time to look over proposals and respond to emails. Now, he wished he'd driven his own truck.

His chauffeur leaned against the hood, waiting patiently, paid to do whatever Gage wanted.

Gage sighed. He didn't want to show up at the saloon in a limousine, but then he wanted the option of escaping when he felt like it. He faced Coop. "I'll ride with you. I'll let my driver know where he can find us." He'd have his chauffeur park down the road from the saloon, in case he needed a quick getaway.

The transportation settled, the men and Emma piled into the trucks and took off for the Ugly Stick Saloon.

What he hoped to accomplish, Gage hadn't a clue, but being with the Jacobs beat going back to Dallas and his upscale apartment alone and he was still dateless for the charity ball.

CHAPTER 5

STILL TINGLING from her second brief contact with the handsome Austin Tate, Fiona arrived early enough to catch Audrey Anderson before the usual weekend crowd showed up. The Ugly Stick Saloon was the place to be on Friday night when it wasn't football season.

Determined to shake off the residual affect of the man she hadn't expected to run into again, she focused on what she had to do to save the ranch. First, she had to find Audrey Anderson.

The owner of the Ugly Stick Saloon straightened from behind the bar, spotted her and smiled, hurrying to close the distance between them

"Fiona!" Audrey engulfed her in a bone-crushing hug, careful not to squish her growing baby bump between them. "I'm so glad you're back home for good."

"It's so good to be home at last." Audrey always made Fiona feel like an old friend, even though she'd only gotten to know her the few times she'd been able to return to Temptation on holiday from school. "And look at you." Fiona stepped back and admired the woman's flushed cheeks and the gentle swell of her belly. "I didn't know you were pregnant."

Audrey smoothed a hand over her abdomen, a smile curving her pretty mouth. She glowed with good health and happiness.

Fiona's heart squeezed tightly. She hoped some day to be as happily in love as Audrey. And she wanted children, half a dozen or more. Alas, all her future plans for love and her own little family had to go on hold until she solved the problem of the family ranch being in jeopardy of foreclosure.

"So what brings you to the Ugly Stick? Are you here for the line-dancing class? It starts at six o'clock." Audrey checked her watch. "Holy crap! Where's Kendall? She's supposed to be here setting up." She turned toward the back of the bar. "Charli!"

Audrey's perky red-haired assistant manager emerged. "Kendall's sick. She just called in. Does that mean you're taking over the line-dancing class?"

Audrey shook her head. "I can't. Libby's out as well. I'll be tending bar tonight. Can't you do it?"

Charli held up her hands. "I don't know any line dances. The best I can do is pole dancing."

"Think the usual crowd for the classes would like a pole-dancing class?" Audrey asked, her face pinched, looking a little desperate.

Charli coughed and gave Audrey a twisted grimace. "And, Audrey, I hate to say it, but I think I'm coming down with whatever Libby and Kendall have."

"Oh, dear." Audrey rubbed a hand over her belly and chewed on her bottom lip. "You'd better leave right now. I don't want everyone else to get sick."

"I can stay until I stock the bar," Charli offered.

"No. Please. Let me rephrase that. I don't want to get sick." She winked at Charli. "Go home, have some hot soup and go to bed. I can manage."

"You're six months pregnant. How are you going to manage with most of your staff out sick?"

"I'll manage," Audrey said.

"Maybe I can help." Fiona hadn't been to a bar to dance since her sophomore year in college, but she was sure she could remember movements to one or two of her favorite line dances. If not, she'd make up some new ones. And this was her chance to prove she could be useful at the Ugly Stick Saloon where the cowboys tipped generously. "I could teach a line dance or two," she offered.

Audrey's eyes brightened. "Can you?" The owner of the saloon hugged her again. "You're hired."

"As a matter of fact," Fiona chewed her bottom lip and then jumped in, "I came to see if you needed a waitress. I'm still applying for teaching positions that won't start until the fall. We—I could use the work until then, and even after I start teaching."

"I definitely need you. My usual staff has come down with something they seem to be sharing. So for sure tonight, and probably through the weekend I could use the extra hand. Between you, me, Lacy and Isabella, we might survive the evening."

"Thank you." Fiona released the breath she'd been

holding. "And if you know of any day jobs available, I could sure use the extra cash, and I like to stay busy."

"Right off the top of my head, I don't know of any. But I can ask around." Audrey nodded toward the stage where the DJ equipment was set up. "You can look through music over the next fifteen minutes. There are usually ten to fifteen people who show up for the Friday night lessons. They like to warm up for later."

While Fiona chose music, she pulled out her smart phone and googled line dancing, settling on two that looked familiar, and refreshed her memory. By the time the students trickled in, she had the movements down and pulled off a fun-filled hour of lessons.

The music, fellowship and exercise helped to push Austin out of her mind for an entire hour. At the end of the lessons, the Friday night regulars drifted in, filling the tables, ordering drinks faster than she and the other waitresses could keep up. The noise and the bustle made her forget, for a moment, the strong attraction she'd felt for the man she'd bumped into in the elevator in Dallas. What were the odds that the same man would show up as the blind date Leslie's system had churned out?

Oh well, it wasn't as if she'd see him again. She'd been pretty discouraging and she really didn't have time. Working at the Ugly Stick, the ranch and any other job she could find would eat up every hour of her days and evenings. She didn't have time for dating, relationships, sex or love.

SITTING in the back seat with Ace, Gage wondered what the hell he was doing. He'd worked hard to rise above his humble beginnings from living in a ramshackle trailer in a Podunk town to amassing a fortune and several elegant townhouses and homes across the country. Going to a country saloon seemed almost a step backward in his charge forward.

At least the paparazzi wouldn't think to look for him there. Arriving in Ace's truck would help as well.

As Ace pulled into the gravel parking lot, Gage could hear the music before he opened the truck doors. The ramshackle building bore a big sign announcing it as the Ugly Stick Saloon. He opened the door to a shout that shook the structure's tin roof.

"Bullshit!"

He recognized the vibrating song through the tin walls as the lively Cotton-eyed Joe, a poignant reminder of his college days at Texas A&M. He and his small, tight group of friends managed a night out when they weren't working part-time jobs or studying for finals.

Coop clapped him on his back. "Brings back some good memories, doesn't it?"

Gage nodded, his chest tightening. The memories were of a time when they were all flat broke.

And look at them now. Not only were they millionaires, they'd blown past millions and headed straight for billions. Never again would they be forced to eat peanut butter sandwiches for weeks because they couldn't afford anything else.

The sound of the music took him back to that time when he'd scrounged up enough money for the cover charge at a country western dancehall, but couldn't afford a drink once inside. Coop had spotted him the only beer he'd had that night, and he'd hated drinking it knowing he couldn't afford to buy it for himself.

He didn't actually know how easy he had it then. Back then, he'd known exactly who he could trust. Since he'd crossed the millionaire threshold, he'd been bombarded by every kind of scammer, con artist and petty thief. Then there were the socially elite who smiled to his face and talked trash behind his back. That included his former fiancée, Lacy. Thankfully, he could still count on his original group of friends.

Inside, the bar was hopping with patrons and a busy staff hurrying with laden trays filled with tall beers and whiskey shots. The dance floor was full, but as the Cotton-eyed Joe ended, a dozen couples hurried back to their tables breathing hard and grinning.

Gage searched the crowd for the pretty redhead with the green eyes and serious expression. At first, he didn't recognize her when he spotted her waiting on a table. Her broad smile practically lit the room and dancing green eyes sparkled as she laughed at what the man seated at the table was saying. She handed him a beer and hugged him before moving on to the next table where she took an order and spun toward the bar.

Another waitress passed in front of him, wearing the shorter-than-short shorts, tank top and cowboy boots, similar to what Fiona had left her house in. In the bar setting, the clothing made more sense, kind of a uniform of sorts.

Emma spoke to a woman with strawberry blond hair and a distinctive baby bump hurrying past, and she pointed toward the tables near to where Fiona had been working. With a nod and a smile, Emma set off, weaving her way through the crowded room to a table being vacated by several cowboys who were finishing their beers and shaking hands.

Cooper followed Emma, and the rest of Emma's brothers either fell in line or found old friends to stop and talk to. The Jacobs family was obviously well known at the Ugly Stick Saloon. People shouted hello as Emma sailed by, smiling and waving as she went.

Gage wasn't exactly sure what he hoped to accomplish at the saloon. He especially wasn't sure why he was drawn to a woman who clearly wanted nothing to do with him. For a moment, he considered leaving. At this point, hiring an escort service to fill his need for a date to the ball would simplify his life. Pursuing Fiona McKenzie had complicated written all over it.

Gage almost turned around and headed back out the door when Coop hooked his arm and turned him to face the strawberry blonde.

"Audrey, this is my friend Austin. Austin, this is Audrey Anderson, owner of the Ugly Stick Saloon."

Audrey took his hand and gave it a firm shake. "Glad to meet you." She winked and tipped her head toward Emma and her brothers. "You keep good company."

He shook the owner's hand. "Nice to meet you, ma'am."

She laughed and pulled him in for a hearty hug. "Don't be such a stranger. And let me tell you a secret. If I wasn't already married to the handsomest cowboy in all of Texas, and carrying his baby," she patted the swell of her belly, "I'd have gone after one of the Jacobs men."

She glanced around. "But don't let Jackson hear me saying that. He can be very jealous when he wants to be."

Gage liked her already. Her warm smile and happy face made him feel welcome in a barroom full of strangers.

"So this is your first time to the Ugly Stick?" She glanced around at the waitresses. "We have just about any kind of beer you could want and the wait staff gives a show every so often. Stick around, you might just have a good time." She winked.

"Thank you, ma'am," he said, again.

Coop spoke up. "Actually, we brought Gage so that he could check out your newest waitress, Fiona McKenzie. They were supposed to be on a date tonight. But things didn't quite work out."

Audrey's brows puckered. "Is that so? Fiona came in asking for a job. Had I known she was supposed to go out tonight, I wouldn't have had her start right away, although heaven knows I need the help. My assistant manager, bar tender and one of my other waitresses are out sick. I wasn't sure how I'd manage until Fiona offered to help out. I'll be sure to carve out a little time for you two to catch at least a dance or two."

Before Gage could protest that he wasn't there to chase after a woman who obviously didn't want to date him, a waitress at the bar shouted, "Audrey! Need another bottle of JD Whiskey!"

"Got it, Lacy!" Audrey smiled. "That's my cue to get back to the bar. Have a seat and sit a spell. A waitress will be get your order." Then she was gone.

Coop grinned. "I don't know where that woman gets

all her energy. I understand she used to be a stripper, saved up all her money to buy this place and hasn't looked back since."

Emma smiled. "Audrey is one of a kind. And all that dancing she did kept her in great shape. She and Jackson were meant for each other and they tried really hard to get pregnant. I'm so happy for them."

"We were meant for each other." Coop winked at Emma. "Leslie's system said so."

Emma hooked her arm through Coop's and hugged him. "Yes, we were, and yes it did."

"I just had to convince you to see that."

She leaned up on her toes. "I'm glad you didn't give up on me."

"Never. I could tell you were special from the moment we met."

Emma and Coop's display of affection left Gage feeling like he was missing out on something. Apparently it hadn't been smooth sailing for Coop and Emma in the beginning, but they were sickeningly happy now. And from all appearances, Emma really loved Coop. She and her brothers had their own ranch, their own money. Emma loved Coop for himself.

A rare instance, Gage told himself.

Gage scratched his head. With Coop and Emma occupied with each other, and the Jacobs brothers engaged with friends, now would be a good time to slip out and forget about Fiona. Yet he found himself following Cooper to the table full of Jacobs men. Perhaps it was to recapture the more innocent times of his college years or maybe it was because he wanted to study the woman who'd turned down a date with him to start a job at the saloon.

After years of every woman he met catering to his slightest whims, Gage was intrigued by the one who hadn't batted an eye at turning him down for a date. Then again, she didn't know he had millions, a chauffeur on standby and everything money could buy. If nothing else, the challenge intrigued him.

Gage took a seat next to Emma, Coop on the other side and three of the four Jacobs brothers scattered around the large table.

When Fiona reached the table, she stared down at the pad in her hand, holding a pen ready. "What can I get y'all?" she asked in a soft southern drawl. She glanced up at the faces around the table and her gaze met his. "You!"

Coop laughed out loud until Emma backhanded him in the gut. He wiped the smile from his face for half a second, before he grinned again.

Heat rose up Gage's neck, but he schooled his expression to the one he used when he sat in negotiations for a buyout. "Miss McKenzie." He nodded. "I'd like a Guinness."

"And maybe a second chance," Ace added. "Whatta ya say, Fi?" Ace, along with Brand, Colton, Cooper and Emma all stared at the poor woman expectantly.

Her body stiffened.

Seeing the frown forming on Fiona's face, Gage shook his head. "Just the Guinness. Nothing else."

With a quick quirk of her lips, she took orders from the others and spun away.

As soon as she was out of earshot, Coop leaned

forward. "Why the hell did you do that? I thought you wanted a date with the woman?"

Gage glanced around the table. "I don't need help getting a date. If Fiona doesn't work out, surely there are other women in the place I can ask." To prove his point he nodded toward a woman working her way through the tables, smiling and laughing. "How about her?"

Ace snorted. "That's Mona Daley." The eldest Jacobs man nodded toward the bar. "See that man with the big belt buckle leaning against the barstool? That's Grant Raleigh, one of the best team ropers and bull riders of the decade."

"I've heard of him," Gage said.

Ace tipped his cowboy hat back on his head. "Yeah, well he and Mona are a thing."

Not willing to give up yet, Gage glanced at the woman joining Mona. "What about that one?"

Brand leaned back his arms crossing over his chest. "That's Bunny. She's taken by not one, but two cowboys. I'm sure they'd put up a fight over her."

Gage's eyes widened. "Two cowboys?"

"Yup."

Two cowboys. Things were different in Temptation, Texas. "Surely not all the women are taken?"

"Damned near," Colton groused. "Seems we need to import more women into the area. We have plenty of cowboys."

Fiona returned with their order and had to stand near enough to Gage to set his Guinness on the table in front of him.

The heat from her body and the scent of honeysuckle surrounded him. All he had to do was turn and his face would be on level with her breasts. Gage's groin tightened. He curled his hand around the chilled bottle of beer to remind him that the woman wasn't interested.

"Can I get y'all anything else?" she asked, her gaze shifting to him and sliding away immediately, the color in her cheeks rising.

Interesting.

Gage was good at reading body language. Her cheeks hadn't reddened until she'd glance at him. If he was a betting man, he'd wager she was a lot more aware of him than she let on.

He held up his beer. "I'll take another in about thirty minutes."

She nodded and left, weaving through the tables, her rounded bottom enticing in the tight denim shorts with the frayed edges.

Shifting in his seat, Gage downed a long swallow of beer and glanced around the saloon.

The band announced a break and music blared from the jukebox. Audrey climbed up on the bar, with help from a tall, dark-haired man who frowned even as he helped the pregnant woman onto the counter. He handed her a microphone, and she smiled at him and winked before addressing the audience. "Ladies and gentleman, it's time for a little Ugly Stick Saloon fun!"

The waitresses ditched their trays and climbed up next to Audrey.

The one Ace had identified as Mona took the microphone from Audrey. "We'll take it from here, sweetie. Jackson, help your pregnant wife down while we crank up the heat in this place." She narrowed her eyes and then pointed across the room at Fiona. "We'd like to introduce you to one of the newest members of our staff here at the Ugly Stick."

Fiona shook her head, her eyes rounding, her hands held up as if to ward off whatever came next.

Mona wasn't backing off. "Give it up for Fiona McKenzie!"

A roar of yee-haws rose from the patrons, Colton, Brand, Ace and every other cowboy and cowgirl in the place shouted, whistled and clapped as Fiona was dragged to the bar and hoisted up to stand beside Mona, her cheeks flaming red.

Mona laughed. "I believe Fiona is a little shy. Didn't Audrey warn you that part of the fun of working here is providing a little entertainment every once in a while?"

"I don't know your dances," Fiona protested.

"No worries, follow along and make up moves of your own. These guys aren't picky as long as you put your heart and your hips into it. Are you, fellas?" She smiled at the crowd and the men roared again.

Gage leaned back in his chair, tapping his cell phone on the table, enjoying the consternation on Fiona's face. He liked that she was uncomfortable and he waited for her to cry uncle and jump down off the bar.

Fiona stared out across the saloon, her gaze landing on him.

Gage crossed his arms and raised his brows in challenge. "She won't do it," he said to Coop, shaking his head.

"Wanna bet?" Coop countered.

Fiona's eyes narrowed and her chin tilted upward.

Music blared over the loud speaker and the song "Save a Horse, Ride a Cowboy" came on.

Mona and Bunny danced in unison with Fiona following along awkwardly, always kicking her boots a step behind the others.

Gage's lips curled into a smile.

When Fiona looked up and caught him grinning, she straightened and gave up trying to follow the other two. Instead, she did her own dance, twisting her hips right and left, dropping lower and then back up. She raised her arm over her head like she was swinging a lasso, the motion emphasizing the swell of her breasts. Her movements were smooth, sexy and completely captivated Gage.

By the time the song ended, he was leaning forward, his gaze locked on Fiona's beautiful body.

Along with every other cowboy in the joint.

Hats rose in the air and the hoots and hollers raised the rooftops.

"I thought you might like our gal Fiona," Mona said. "Now grab your own gal and get to dancin'! We have a lot more beer and whiskey comin' your way to cool you off or get you fired up."

A lively song came on and half of the patrons of the saloon headed for the dance floor, smiling, laughing and having a good time.

Coop nudged Gage's arm. "Audrey encourages her waitresses to dance with the customers if they like. Why don't you go ask Fiona?"

Ace's lips twisted. "If you don't, I will. That gal's got some moves." He started to rise, but Gage beat him to it.

"I guess it's worth a second chance," he muttered, more to himself than to the others at his table.

"That's the spirit!" Brandon clapped him on the back. "Go get 'er. And I'll be right behind you when she turns you down." He stood and would have followed, if Ace hadn't stuck out an arm, clothes-lining him across the chest. "Let Gage have his shot."

Brandon shoved his brother's arm aside. "I was kidding. There's a pretty little thing sitting at the corner of the bar. I thought I'd rescue her from Tye Wilson. He's headed her way now to ask her to dance and the poor kid has two left feet."

Gage barely heard the conversation as he walked away from the Jacobs' table. His gaze and concentration rested on Fiona as she climbed down from the bar with the help of Audrey's husband.

When she finally looked up, Gage stood in front of her. "Would you care to dance?"

She frowned. "I have to work."

He gave her a crooked grin. "Consider it a consolation prize for standing me up on our first date."

"I told you, I didn't make the date. You'll have to take it up with my sisters."

"Okay, don't consider it a consolation prize. Call it a pity dance. If you don't dance with me, I have to go back to a table full of cowboys who will give me hell for getting shut down twice in one night by the prettiest girl in the saloon."

Fiona shook her head. "Is that all you've got?"

Gage shrugged. "Yeah. My reputation and manhood are on the line."

"I'm sure you'll live." She reached for her tray, but

Gage blocked her path and took her hand in his, raising it to his lips.

For some reason he really wanted her to dance with him, and he wasn't going back to his table until she agreed. He drew in a breath and said softly, "Please."

CHAPTER 6

FIONA FROZE, her heart stopping as she racked her brain for words, any excuse not to dance with the man who'd stolen her breath away in the elevator in Dallas. She'd avoided him at her house by running out the door before she got too close.

Serving his beer, she'd almost bumped into him. She'd been near enough she could smell his cologne, and she'd nearly leaned into him to get an even better whiff. Fiona jerked her hand free of his, and had it on the tip of her tongue to reiterate that she couldn't dance with him because she had to work.

As Fiona opened her mouth, Audrey chose that moment to walk by. "Oh, Fiona. Had I known you were supposed to be on a date tonight, I wouldn't have dragged you into working." She lifted Fiona's hand and Austin's and put them together again.

A blast of electricity shot up her arm and spread white-hot heat throughout her body. If his fingers hadn't closed around hers, she'd have jerked her hand away again.

"Go on, you two have a dance. Heck, if I didn't need your help so badly tonight, Fiona, I'd say take off." Audrey grimaced. "But I need you. So dance, but don't leave yet. Not until the rush is over, please."

"A dance isn't necessary." Fiona found her tongue. "I wouldn't dream of taking time for myself when you're so shorthanded."

"We'll work a few minutes around a dance or two." Audrey waved her hands. "Go on, you two. The least you can do is give the poor man a dance, since I ruined your plans." A shout drew Audrey's attention. "Gotta go. Someone must have ordered a mixed drink and Mona's strictly beer and whiskey." The pregnant bar owner hurried off to take up her duties mixing drinks, freeing Mona to head back out onto the floor to fill orders.

Fiona tried to free her hand, but Austin wasn't letting go. "Okay. One dance and you have to give back my hand. I'll need it to wait tables."

"One dance," he agreed, his voice as sexy as the rest of him. Fiona feared she was going to be in big trouble. She could hope the music stayed lively precluding them from actually touching.

As Austin led her toward the dance floor, the music changed from a fast-paced two-step to a belly-rubbin' slow dance. Fiona swallowed her groan that morphed into a moan as the man enveloped her in his arms, tugging her close, his hands resting low on her back, pressing her hips against his.

This was what Fiona had wanted to avoid. The first time she'd been in his arms had left her breathless. Now his heat, the cologne, the hard expanse of muscle pressed to her breasts and the harder bulge nudging her belly, made her knees weak and her brain matter turn to goo.

She didn't need this now when her family was in dire straits. They stood to lose the only home she'd ever known and all the memories she had of her dear mother with it.

All those thoughts faded away in a fog of lust as she melted against Austin. His hands slid lower into the back pockets of her cutoff shorts.

He didn't speak, he didn't say anything, just held her and swayed to the haunting love song, his cheek pressed to the side of her hair.

For three minutes, every other thought, person or memory disappeared while she danced with Austin.

When the song ended, they rocked back and forth for a good twenty seconds longer, before Austin stopped and tipped her chin upward. "Thank you." Then, before Fiona could gather her wits, he bent and brushed his lips across hers, sending electric tingles all the way to her toes.

As quickly as his lips touched, Austin drew away and smiled. "I believe Audrey is looking a little desperate."

"Oh my God." Fiona spun and raced toward the back of the saloon, dodging between customers. She ran into two or three cowboys along the way, excused herself and kept running until she reached the bar.

Audrey grinned. "Glad you got some time with your cowboy. He seemed nice enough and oh so sexy."

"I barely know him," Fiona muttered, her lips still tingling from the kiss.

"I think he'd like to know you a lot better." Audrey winked and nodded toward the tray on the counter. "That goes to table six. You better hurry before they start hollerin'."

Thankful for the hard work to keep her from thinking about Austin Tate, Fiona hoisted the tray onto her shoulder and carried it to the table full of cowboys in the far corner. For one whole minute, she had her back to the man who'd turned her knees to pudding and made her heart thud so hard against her ribs Fiona thought for sure the patrons of the Ugly Stick would hear it over the music.

When she returned to the bar, she caught Mona on her way out to her tables.

"Switch tables with me," Fiona begged.

Mona frowned. "Why?"

"I just need you to switch with me." She reached out for the tray. "Please."

Mona shrugged. "You're giving up the Jacobs?" The other waitress snorted. "It's your lost tip money, but I'm game. I get better tips from them than my customers at the beauty shop."

Fiona delivered the tray of drinks Mona had earmarked for another table on the opposite side of the saloon from the Jacobs brothers and Austin Tate. For the rest of the evening she avoided running into Austin, avoided smelling his cologne and, most of all, avoiding throwing herself into his arms and begging him to kiss her again. Only this time, she wanted a real kiss.

Hells bells! She didn't have time to mess around with a charming, sexy cowboy. All her waking hours would be full to overflowing with work, work and more work until she made enough money to dig the family home out of the debt they were in.

She prayed it wouldn't be too little too late. What she really needed was to win the lottery or find a prince charming who wanted to swoop his Cinderella off her tired feet and save her family from losing their home.

Fiona snorted. Not that she was Cinderella. She loved her stepsisters and her dearly departed stepmother, unlike the fairytale counterpart. And her father was very much alive and well. She didn't need someone to rescue her, either. She'd always loved a challenge and she was used to solving her own problems. This one was just a little bigger than anything else she'd encountered while going to college. She had no doubt she could handle it.

Giving herself a firm shake, she got back to work, smiled big, flirted with the customers and raked in the tips. At the end of the night, she might have enough money to pay the electric bill. A few more nights like this and she might have enough to pay the fee for her sisters' state board exams.

Forcing back the feeling of being one lone life raft in a raging sea, she waited one table at time, served one beer at a time and focused on the things she *could* control.

Her feelings and desires for Austin Tate were out of her control and to be avoided at all costs.

Coop nudged Gage with his elbow. "I thought for sure you and Fiona had a moment there on the dance floor. Did you do something to piss her off?"

Gage frowned at the auburn-haired beauty working an entirely different section of tables since they'd danced. What had gone wrong? Like Coop said, he'd thought they'd had a connection. After only the first few beats of the music, Fiona's body had melted into his, her arms circled his neck, and she'd clung to him until well after the last note had been played and the next song kicked in.

He'd been so convinced she'd felt the same way, he'd stolen a brief kiss.

Had he known it would make her switch tables...

Hell, he'd have kissed her all over again. Only this time, he'd have kissed her harder, longer and deeper. She'd have a damn good reason to be mad.

As it was, he was still scratching his head at her deliberate attempt to avoid him.

He'd been confused, then angry and now resigned. If she didn't want to be with him, he shouldn't care. Move on. Find another woman.

The trouble was, no other woman in the saloon, or in Dallas, for that matter, made him want to pursue her like Fiona.

Her lips had been soft and tasted of cherry Chapstick. Her breasts had pressed against him, the tips, hard little buttons, peaked through her bra and the fabric of her tank top. How he'd wanted to taste them next.

The more she ignored him, the more he wanted to confront her for a reason why. But the only way to do that would be to wait until he could catch herby herself. In a saloon full of thirsty, horny cowboys getting drunker by the minute, getting her alone was not likely.

Gage tapped his cell phone against the table and it vibrated in his hand.

He frowned as a text message popped up on the screen from William Langley.

Call me

His pulse leaped. Had Langley finally made up his mind? Was he going to sell the property to Gage or turn him down? His finger on the button to call, Gage glanced around. Band members were tuning their guitars, ready to play another set. If he wanted to talk to Langley, he'd have to step outside.

Excusing himself, he left the bar and walked out into the gravel parking lot and dialed William Langley's number. This could be it. Langley could be calling him to say he would sell the property to him.

"Tate?" Langley barked into Gage's ear.

"Yes, sir."

"My daughter and I are hosting a barbeque out at the ranch tomorrow. I'd like you to come."

Gage almost groaned. "You and Priscilla?"

"She's the only daughter I have. Yes, Priscilla. And a few other guests."

"I had planned on spending Saturday at one of my job sites."

"It will give us an uninterrupted opportunity to discuss your plans for the corner of Elm and Griffin."

Had it been just him and Langley, Gage would have jumped at the offer. The problem was Priscilla. What hell was the woman planning now? He couldn't say no if this were the only other chance he'd have to meet with Langley before he made his final decision. Being invited to Langley's home where Priscilla was likely to stake her claim on him wasn't good. Should he make Priscilla mad, it could count against him in William Langley's books. Hell, he had to go. His only other alternative was to make Priscilla believe he was taken. "I'd love to come, but my plan for work at the site included my girlfriend. Do you mind if I bring her?"

"Not at all. I'll take that as a yes, then. Oh, and Tate, be prepared to stay the night. It's too far out to return to Dallas the same day. Do you need me to send my plane to pick up you and your girl?"

He hadn't considered distance. In his research, he'd discovered Langley owned property all over Texas, several other states and in other countries. The man liked collecting real estate like some men collected coins. "No need to send your plane. I'll take mine. All I need are the coordinates."

"I'll have my pilot forward those to you tonight. The festivities begin at five o'clock. That should give you plenty of time to get here and get settled."

"Thank you for the invitation, Mr. Langley. I look forward to further discussion about the property in Dallas."

The call ended as abruptly as it began. Langley didn't say goodbye, safe travels or kiss my ass. He'd just hung up once he'd secured Gage's commitment to be there.

Gage slid his phone into his pocket, his mind going to the next day and what he'd say to Langley to get him to sell that property to him. He paced to the end of the Ugly Stick Saloon and continued around to the back of the building. Several laps around the saloon and he knew what he would say, had a counter for every argument and would be ready for anything William Langley had to throw at him.

In the middle of an internal sales pitch, he remembered the one kink in the plan. Priscilla. The woman knew how to manipulate her father. If she thought for a moment Gage was available, she'd be on him like a fly on a picnic ham. Bringing a girlfriend along was the only way he could think of to keep Priscilla at bay.

But who could he take as a girlfriend? It couldn't be just anyone. The woman had to be able to stand up to Priscilla, and yet not offend the woman and her father.

As he rounded to the back of the building for the third time, the rear exit door opened and a female figure stood silhouetted in the dull yellow glow of the porch light. She turned and backed down the steps, dragging a heavy garbage bag. Once she got it through the door, she straightened, pressing her hands to the base of her spine.

As she lifted her head the yellow light above the back porch, shone down in her face.

Fiona.

She closed her eyes and sighed, then bent to lift the heavy bag, slinging it around and over her shoulder. She staggered sideways a few steps then hunched and trudged toward the big trash bin on the corner of the back parking area.

Just the person he wanted to see. As well rehearsed as he was for his sales pitch with Langley, he was completely at a loss for what he'd say to Fiona to get her to go as his girlfriend to an overnight event on the Langley ranch.

Gage hurried forward and grabbed the bag as she reached the bin.

Fiona jumped back with a startled yelp. "Oh!" She drew in a deep breath and let it out. "It's you. You scared the bejeezus out of me."

"I'm sorry. I didn't mean to, but when I saw you carrying that heavy bag, I thought I could be of assistance."

Her eyes flared and, for a moment, he thought she might smile. As quickly as that thought came and went, her lips thinned and she hitched the bag up higher. "I can manage on my own, thank you."

"At least let me help get it over the edge." Again, he reached for the bag.

Fiona backed a step. "I don't need your help."

The woman was damned stubborn. Gage crossed his arms. "Okay." He'd wait until she had the bag in the container until he asked her if she'd consider going with him the next day. The odds that she'd say yes were pretty slim. But he didn't have a lot of choices or time.

CHAPTER 7

Fiona's feet hurt, her back ached and the trash smelled to high heaven, making her want to gag, and Mr. Dreamypants wasn't making it any easier. With the heavy bag of garbage cutting into her shoulder, she frowned at him. "Aren't you going back inside?"

"No." He shook his head. "I'm enjoying the fresh air."

With a snort, she turned her back to the bin and pressed the bag against it. "Fresh air near the trash? Yeah, right." She'd handled hay bales heavier than this one bag. But unlike a solid bale of hay, the bag contents of the trash bag shifted every time she pushed against it.

Once she had it firmly against the metal container, she turned, keeping her body against the bag to keep it from sliding to the ground. Rethinking her decision to be tough and handle the trash on her own, she put her shoulder into the bag and shoved it upward. As it reached the rip of the container, the plastic material of the bag caught on the edge and refused to go any farther.

Frustration burned deep in Fiona's chest. She refused to admit defeat in front of the handsome man standing close enough she could see the moonlight shining in his blue eyes. Why couldn't he go away and let her take care of the humiliating task of hefting a bag bigger than she was into the trash bin?

She gritted her teeth, bent her knees and gave a good, angry shove. That damned bag was going in!

The plastic clung to the edge for a moment longer then shot upward, the sharp edge of the bin ripping a hole in the side of the bag. Instead of tipping into the metal container, the bag exploded, raining whiskey bottles, half-empty beer bottles, soggy nachos and left-over food items down over Fiona.

A whiskey bottle conked her head, and she swayed, tears filling her eyes. "Well, damn!"

Austin Tate hurried forward.

"Don't you dare laugh," she grumbled, pulling a wet napkin out of her beer-soaked hair.

"I wouldn't dare." His eyes twinkled and his jaw twitched.

Damn him. Fiona could tell Austin was fighting the urge.

Finally, he burst out laughing at the same time as he pulled her into his arms. "Oh, sweetheart, you are a mess."

"You shouldn't. I stink to high heaven." But his hands were insistent, pulling her against his chest. She leaned into him, her head aching, her feet hurting worse and her entire body smelling of beer, cheese and yuck. "You're going to get stuff all over you."

"I can take a bath and wash my clothes later. Let me help you."

Then before she could form another protest, he bent and scooped bottles, cups and trash into the destroyed bag.

Fiona dropped down on her haunches and helped, their heads within inches of each other. "Thanks. I should have let you help when it wasn't such a big mess."

He winked at her. "I like a feisty female."

She tossed a bottle over her shoulder into the bin. "You mean stubborn."

"No, I stand by feisty." When all the trash had been thrown into the container, he straightened and brushed his hands together.

Without trash between them, Fiona suddenly felt exposed and every bit aware of her short shorts and the broad expanse of Austin's chest. If she weren't smelling like beer and covered in catsup and nacho cheese, she'd be tempted to kiss him for helping her. "At the very least, come through the back door and wash up before you go back to your friends." She started for the back door but a hand gripped her arm and pulled her to a stop.

"Wait." Austin turned her to face him.

He had catsup on his shirt, and Fiona tried to focus on it, but his gaze drew hers. "Thanks for helping me clean up."

The man leaned toward her, his full lips only inches from hers. Remembering the kiss on the dance floor, Fiona swayed toward him.

"You missed a spot." He reached up and plucked a wet napkin from her hair and tossed it in the bin.

Her breathing uneven, and her lips tingling, heat rose in Fiona's cheeks. Why she thought the man would kiss her when she smelled like something her barn cat dragged in, she didn't know. She took a step backward, putting space and sanity between them. "Again, thanks. Maybe I could buy you a beer for your trouble."

"I don't need another beer. There's something else I want instead."

His voice melted over her like warm chocolate. Fiona let it sink into her pores before his words registered. "Whiskey? Rum?" Her voice faded at the intensity of his gaze.

"I want you," he said.

"Me?" she squeaked. Her core tightened and her heart stuttered for several beats before it raced ahead. She pictured the two of them lying naked in the sheets, doing unimaginable things, each of them involving hot sex, groping hands and sweat. When she remembered to breathe again, her brows lowered. Did he think she was easy or into one-night stands? For a moment, the thought intrigued her. A one-night stand with the handsome Austin Tate might not be all that bad. But she wasn't that kind of girl. "I'm sorry. You must have the wrong idea about me."

He chuckled again, making her want to fish one of the bottles out of the trash and hit him with it. "I don't think I'm handling this well. What I want is for you to come with me to a barbeque on a business acquaintance's ranch tomorrow."

"A barbeque?" Grilled steaks and chicken didn't evoke the same images, and brought Fiona back to reality. "I'm sorry. I have to work tomorrow."

"Can't you take off one day? I'd love for you to come." He took her dirty hand in his equally dirty one. "We could get to know each other better."

He could have coaxed a saint out of her panties when he spoke in those low sexy tones. And he almost had her agreeing to hand over her panties, until she remembered why she was working. "I can't. I need the work." The money she could earn meant the difference between making the next mortgage payment or putting food on the table and being foreclosed on and evicted. "Some of us have to earn a living."

When she tried to pull her hands free, his fingers tightened on hers.

"If it's about money, I'll pay you to come with me."

"Pay me to go to a barbeque with you?" This time when she jerked her hands away, he let go. "What, like an escort service?"

He shrugged. "Yeah, sure."

She shook her head. "Not interested. Again, I'm not that kind of girl."

"I'm not asking for sex. I need a date."

She crossed her arms and raked her gaze from the top of his head to the tips of his cowboy boots. "You need a date." Her snort was anything but ladylike and she didn't care. "You could walk into that bar and whistle, and any female would come running."

"I don't want any female. I want you."

"And we're back to, I'm. Not. For. Sale." She turned away and stalked to the rear entrance of the saloon.

"Please, hear me out," he said, hurrying after her.

Fiona spun to face him and he almost plowed into her. "You just asked me out on a paid date." She threw her hand in the air, struggling for words. "I don't even know how to respond to that."

"By saying yes. I'll make it worth your time." He pulled his wallet out and took out ten one hundred dollar bills. "One thousand enough?"

She couldn't lie to herself. A thousand dollars would go a long way... Fiona shook herself. "Seriously? Just how desperate are you?"

His lips twisted. "You have no idea."

She planted her fists on her hips. "Enlighten me." The she shook herself. "On second thought. Don't. I'm not even considering this. The money I earn is from hard work, not whatever you have in mind." Again, she spun and reached for the handle to the back door. The door was locked. "Great. Just freakin' great."

A hand descended on her shoulder and pushed her around, pressing her back to the door. "For your information, I am not offering to pay you for sex." Austin glared down at her as he stood on the back porch, his big body overpowering her. "You're right. I can have any woman I want at the snap of my fingers."

"I said whistle," she muttered.

"Whatever. I don't want any woman. I need someone who's smart, passably pretty and can hold her own against a spoiled rich girl. I thought that might be you." His voice dropped to a bone-melting whisper. "Apparently, I was wrong." He leaned closer, his lips nearly touching hers.

Fiona stiffened, her gaze slipping to those lips that had teased her earlier into thinking she might like to have another taste.

"I offered to pay for that date only because you seemed to be in need of the money that working tomorrow would bring. I don't normally have to buy a date. I only suggested it to make the decision easier." He leaned closer, his lips skimming past her cheek to her earlobe. "For the record, if I wanted to have sex with you, I wouldn't have to pay."

The warmth of his breath on her ear made her tilt her head ever so slightly to the side, giving him better access to her throat. Her heart stopped and she waited for his mouth to touch her. Anywhere would be fine.

Instead, he whispered in that deep, rich tone, "I know how to make a woman beg for it," he said. "You'd be no different."

She jerked back and swung her hand hard, her palm connecting with his cheek in a loud, smack.

Austin stepped down from the porch, his back ramrod straight, the yellow light revealing a bright red handprint on his face.

Fiona clamped her hand to her mouth, horrified she had hit the man, yet she refused to apologize. He had no right to stir her up and then blatantly insult her. She was not one of his women who'd apparently drop their panties as soon as he touched them. No matter how wet hers had become by just being near him. Damn him to hell!

"I see you need time to think about my proposal. And I'll be clear: no sex, just be my date for the barbeque and evening activities. I'll pay you one thousand dollars up front. If you last through the event without slapping me again, I'll pay you another thousand dollars. That's two thousand dollars and you don't even have to get naked." He paused, his eyes narrowing slightly. "Unless you want to."

"You can take your offer straight to hell with you." She turned and banged on the back door. When no one came, she marched down the steps, her head held high, and passed him without looking at the red mark on his face or the smug look curling his lips. The man was impossible. And she would never consider going out with him with or without the two grand he'd just offered.

She hadn't quite gotten past him when he said, "And, Fiona, I'll need your answer by eight o'clock in the morning."

Fiona faced him, her lips pressed into a thin line, her fists clenched at her sides to keep from hitting him again. "I can tell you now—"

Without warning, he pulled her to him. He kissed her lips, stealing her words and her breath. Then he smiled down at her. "Don't decide now. I can see you're still upset. Take your time and think about it." Austin turned and walked away, leaving her standing in the faint glow from the light over the back porch. Too soon, he disappeared into the shadows.

For a long moment, she stared into the darkness, wondering if she'd dreamed up the whole encounter with Austin Tate. The sting on her palm told her otherwise and made her bite her bottom lip guiltily. Absently, she rubbed her hand on the side of her shorts as she rehashed his invitation.

Hell, if she hadn't needed to work, she might have gone with him to the barbeque, before he'd offered to pay her to go with him. What kind of man paid for a date?

Feeling righteous about her reaction to his invitation, Fiona walked around the opposite side of the building to the front entrance and slipped past Greta Sue the bouncer. A few minutes in the bathroom assured her she looked as bad as she smelled. And Austin had asked her to go with him to a barbeque. He must have thought her pathetic to offer to pay for her to go. Especially as awful as she looked.

Fiona scrubbed the garbage from her face, and ducked her head under the water to rinse the beer and other nastiness out of her hair. When she felt sufficiently clean, she squeezed the excess water out of her hair, ran a comb through it, dried her hands and went back to work. No matter how much she scrubbed, she couldn't wash the tingling off her lips where he'd kissed her, nor could she dislodge the heat simmering in her core every time she thought about Austin Tate.

HIS FACE still smarting from the slap he'd earned, Gage walked to the end of the parking lot and texted Coop to let him know he was leaving. Then he called his driver. Within two minutes, he settled into the back seat of the limousine. He poured a healthy dose of the best whiskey money could buy, and drank half of it down before he pressed the button, dropping the darkened panel between the back of the vehicle and the front.

Joe Wallace glanced at him in the rearview mirror. "Sir, do you need anything?"

"Joe, why are women so damned hard to get along with?" he asked, rubbing the side of his cheek.

"Sir, I'm married and I have no problem with my wife."

Gage leaned forward. "How do you manage that?"

Joe smiled into the mirror. "I treat her with the respect she deserves, and love her unconditionally."

Gage scratched his chin. "And that works for you?"

"Most of the time," Joe admitted. "The rest of the time, I let her win the arguments. Choosing your battles is just as important as winning the war. Sometimes to win, you have to forfeit."

"What if you're right?'

"Saying you're sorry goes a long way to soothing the bristles. When I *am* in the right, I give her time to come around."

The problem was, Gage wasn't sorry he'd gotten Fiona mad enough to slap his face. The fire in her pretty green eyes made him want to get her stirred up all over again. When Fiona had pressed her body against his on the dance floor, Gage couldn't deny the heat burning in his belly or that he wanted to hold her closer, feel her skin against his. Though he'd been cocky and told her he could make her beg for his touch, he wasn't so sure now. She'd been pretty adamant she could resist him. And the stubborn redhead probably would, if only to spite him. He prayed that deep down she was just as hot for him as he was for her.

"Anything else, sir?" Joe asked, shaking Gage out of his reverie.

"No, Joe. Thank you." He pressed the button and the partition rose, blocking his view of Joe, giving him the privacy he needed to think through his options for the following day. If he didn't have a date going to the Langley ranch, what was the worst that could happen?

Priscilla could make his life miserable by hanging all over him in front of her father. If he rebuffed Langley's little princess, he could kiss the property he needed goodbye.

So?

He'd come this far without Langley's prime real estate. He'd find another deal and move forward with his plans for Tate Towers, an office complex with a full-scale shopping mall complete with upscale restaurants and any service a wealthy patron could desire. If he had to move it out of the city center, so be it. He just hated to lose this battle because of a woman. Especially one as spoiled as Priscilla.

Gage received the coordinates for Langley's ranch and immediately forwarded them to his assistant, asking him to have his jet fueled, and his flight plan filed with a short stop in Temptation, Texas before he headed to Langley's ranch.

In case Fiona decided to pass on his invitation, Gage spent the remainder of the ride back to Dallas going through the names of all the women he knew. Every one of them would jump at the chance to go with him to Langley's ranch. That wasn't the problem. Cutting them loose afterward made him hesitate. He didn't need any negative trash talk coming back on him.

As with securing a date for the charity ball, he came up empty. If he asked any of the women he knew to go with him to either function, the paparazzi would have him engaged and married before the event was over. If he ditched the woman the next day, he'd be right back to square one with his public image. Gage Tate breaks another heart in Texas.

Joe dropped off Gage in front of the Tate Enterprises office complex. He had the penthouse suite at the very top with a beautiful view of the Dallas skyline. After a short trip in his private elevator to the ninety-second floor, he entered the expansive, marble-tiled foyer of his apartment. Roman columns made of white marble rose toward the high ceiling, bracketing the entrance. The living area was spacious, with floor-to-ceiling windows taking full advantage of the Dallas skyline in the day or at night, facing the west for the best sunsets. When the heat was too much in the summertime, electric shades rolled down over the windows, blocking the heat.

He'd had a top interior designer choose the furnishings and artwork for his apartment. She'd arranged soft, white leather sofas around black onyx tables. Gray, black and white artwork hung on the walls. A couple of throw pillows provided the only splashes of orange, red and blue in the otherwise sterile environment.

Gage entered his bedroom, another large space with rich brown and cream accents and black lacquer furnishings. He undressed, dropping his clothes into a laundry hamper, and stepped into the huge shower, big enough for six people to stand inside comfortably. Water shot at him from multiple directions, gentle as rain from above and pulsing, water jets from the sides. He'd always thought it would be more fun if he had someone to share it. Yet he'd never wanted to bring any of the women he'd dated back to his private space.

For that matter, he didn't spend much time there himself.

He'd felt more at home in the two bedroom apartment he'd lived in up until he could afford to move into the penthouse suite of his newly remodeled building.

Switching off the shower, he reached for a towel and dried his body, then walked naked into his bedroom with the king-sized bed taking center stage. Immediately, he thought of how Fiona's body pressed against him on the dance floor at the Ugly Stick Saloon. He wondered how much better her body would feel pressed against his skin in the smooth sheets of his massive bed. With a groan, he pulled on a pair of boxer shorts and padded barefoot into the living room, forcing his imagination away from a naked redhead.

Instead he replayed mental images of the McKenzie's home with the faded paint and weathered porch. The house needed repairs, much like the homes he'd worked on during the summers between semesters of college. Like those homes, he could tell the McKenzie house had "good bones". All it needed was some tender loving care and an infusion of cash to make it happen.

As quickly as his thoughts ran over the house, he shifted back to Fiona in the living room of her home wearing those impossibly sexy shorts, her long, wet hair hanging down her back, curls springing around her shoulders as they dried. Her fresh, clean face smiling briefly at him as she left the house for work at the Ugly Stick Saloon.

He glanced at the clock on his nightstand. Three o'clock. Five more hours until he'd call Fiona for her final answer. He fully expected her to tell him where he could go with his offer. Touching his hand to his cheek, he grinned. He supposed if he had been in her pretty boots, he'd have slapped his face too. He'd said she was no different than the other women he'd seduced.

But she was different. She wasn't pursuing him—he was pursuing her. Perhaps that was the difference. He was used to having women throw themselves at him.

Too wound up by the events of the night, Gage went to his home office and sat at his drafting table. When he couldn't focus on the day-to-day business of running a billion-dollar company, he returned to what had made him wealthy in the first place—his designs.

After an hour staring at his drafting table, twirling a mechanical pencil between his fingers, he gave up and went to bed, hoping for a few hours sleep. Even this plan was doomed to failure, because every time he closed his eyes, Fiona was there.

CHAPTER 8

FIONA WORKED until two o'clock in the morning when the Ugly Stick Saloon finally closed, sending the last patron home in a sheriff's deputy's vehicle, courtesy of the county.

Audrey had gone home at midnight after announcing to the customers that only beer, wine and whiskey shooters would be served after she left and Mona took over as bartender.

Fiona had smiled as Mona good-naturedly took the ribbing from the locals.

When the last of the chairs were stacked on the tables, she helped mop the floors and took out the trash, determined not to make a mess of it this time. Even though she knew Austin Tate had gone, she couldn't help looking around for him as she dumped the garbage.

She'd had plenty of time to cool down and as tired as she was, she couldn't find the energy to be mad. Disappointed? Yeah. She supposed the connection she'd felt with him on the dance floor had been one-sided. She'd almost reconsidered her refusal to go out with the man.

Making a note to herself to talk to Leslie about the intentions of the clients she hand-selected, Fiona climbed into her father's beat up pickup and twisted the key in the ignition. It didn't start until her third attempt. The old truck had been in the family for over twenty years. She wouldn't have driven it if her own car hadn't bit the dust the week before. Her brother had it in his shop in Temptation, but could do nothing without four thousand dollars for a new engine.

That wasn't an option. Not anytime in the near future. While her brother, Magnus, searched junkyards for another engine he might rebuild for a lot less, she was stuck driving the only other family vehicle.

She pulled out of the parking lot onto the highway and headed away from Temptation to the Rafter M Ranch. Tired to the bone, Fiona couldn't stop thinking about Austin Tate. A mile from the ranch gate, the old truck coughed, belched smoke and the engine died.

"No, no, no!" Fiona steered toward the side of the road, using the remaining momentum to drive the truck off the highway before it stopped completely. She tried to start the engine, but nothing happened, not even a chug or grinding noise.

Fiona leaned her forehead against the steering wheel. What else could go wrong? They didn't have the money to fix her car, they sure as hell didn't have the money to fix the old truck. Resigning herself to sore feet, she climbed down from the truck, slung her purse over her shoulder and walked. What was one more mile to the fifty miles she must have walked waiting tables all night?

Twenty minutes later, she cleared the tree-lined drive and stepped into the open, her home in front of her, every light shining from the windows. What the hell was going on? Had her sisters and father stayed awake to make sure she got home okay?

Dragging herself up the stairs she reached for the front door knob. Before her fingers touched it, the door swung open and Bianca, carrying a bucket full of water, barged through. "Oh, Fiona, we're glad you're here. Grab some towels and start mopping."

"What's going on?" Fiona asked.

"The water heater sprang a leak. All thirty gallons of hot water is filling the hallway, living room and bedrooms. Dad and Brit are moving furniture out of the living room to keep it from being damaged, Magnus is on his way out to help."

Fiona touched her sister's arm. "Mom's antique secretary?"

"It was the first thing out the door." Bianca nodded to the pretty solid mahogany desk on the far end of the porch.

"Thank, God." It was the piece of furniture her mother had loved the most. Her grandmother had handed it down to her mother and her mother to her.

"Dad said the carpet'll be ruined. He's clearing all the furniture out of the living room so he can pull it up."

Her father and Britney appeared in the hallway, one on either end of the couch.

Bianca flung open the front door and held it while the two carried the couch out onto the porch.

Magnus's SUV pulled up the drive and he got out. "We can't catch a break, can we?" After hugging Fiona, he went to work with their father, taking over lifting the heavier items, including an antique curio cabinet and the old upright piano her mother used to play.

Between the five of them, they hauled every piece of furniture out of the living room and put the bedposts in pots and pans to keep the wood from being damaged by the water.

Once the furniture was preserved, they went to work mopping up the water.

By the time the sun rose on the day, they'd pulled up all the carpet, exposing the original wood flooring from when the house had first been built. Thankfully by removing the carpet, the wood would dry on its own.

Bianca and Britney dragged themselves off to bed, and Magnus left for Temptation to open his shop, leaving Fiona and her father to assess the damage.

Her father stood in the middle of the living room. "I hope the floors don't warp."

Fiona slipped an arm around his waist and leaned into him, too tired to think. "If it does, we'll get used to it. Don't worry, Dad. We've been through worse."

"I'm even more convinced we need to sell this place." The lines in her father's face appeared deeper and his shoulders slumped.

"No, Dad. Don't say that. I just got home. Give me a chance to make it work."

He pressed a kiss to the top of her head. "I won't let you work yourself into an early grave trying to take care of us and this albatross of a ranch." He wrinkled is nose and sniffed. "You smell like beer."

"I need a shower." Then she remembered the hot water heater and sighed, pasting a smile on her face when all she wanted to do was cry. "I guess a cold shower is better than nothing until we can afford a new water heater. Go to bed, Dad. Everything will look better after you've had a few hours of sleep."

"I'm not so sure," he muttered, trudging up the stairs to his bedroom.

Fiona took the last of the wet towels outside and draped them over the clothesline. When she returned to the house, the telephone was ringing and nobody was answering. Who could be calling at eight o'clock on Saturday morning?

She lifted the phone, prepared to tell the sales-marketer where he could go.

"Fiona?" the deep, rich tone filled the line and washed over her like warm, sweet chocolate syrup. Her knees nearly buckled and tears filled her eyes.

"This is she," she said, forcing her voice past the lump in her throat. She'd held it together in front of her father, brother and sisters, but hearing Austin's voice, she nearly collapsed with the need to be held in strong arms and reassured that all was not lost.

"Did you make a decision?" he asked.

Then it all came back to her. His invitation, the money he was willing to pay her to be his date and, mostly, what that money would mean to her family. Fiona wanted to tell him no way in hell. But she couldn't. Not with her father's truck stranded on the side of the road, the water heater busted and the mortgage payment past due.

"Two thousand dollars?" she whispered, hating that she would be taking money for a date.

He hesitated, then replied. "Yes."

"Sex isn't required?"

"No sex." He paused. "Unless you want to."

Despite her exhaustion, her treacherous body tingled all over. "No sex," she said, as much for her benefit as his.

"As you wish."

She sagged against the wall, too tired to fight. "What should I wear, and what time are we leaving?"

"My car will pick you up at eleven. Jeans for the day, a dress for the evening as I assume there will be dancing. Oh, and pack an overnight bag."

Her hand tightened on the phone. "Overnight bag? I thought we agreed, no sex."

"We did. But we've been invited to stay overnight. I'll have you back by Sunday evening."

Fiona shook her head, and then realized Austin couldn't see the movement over the phone. "I hardly know you. How can I be sure you aren't taking me to some nudist commune or plan to sell me into the sex trade."

His chuckle warmed her ear and other places farther south. "I promised no sex, unless you want it. And clothes aren't optional where we're going. They're required."

Needing the money as badly as she did, she couldn't turn down the offer. "Just so you know, I'm a black belt in taekwondo."

"I'll try to remember that." He paused. "Eleven?"

"I'll be ready." As she hung up, her hands shook, and

she pressed them to her heated cheeks. She was hiring out as an escort for a date with a man she knew nothing about.

"Who was that?"

Fiona spun to find Bianca leaning against the wall, rubbing her eyes, wearing a babydoll nightgown, her blond hair sticking out.

"Austin Tate," she said, her lips thinning.

Britney padded up behind Bianca, yawning. "Austin Tate?" She blinked and stretched. "Did you change your mind about going out with him?"

Not really, but the events of the previous night forced had her into it. "Yes. We're going to a barbecue."

Bianca clapped her hands. "That's wonderful."

Britney elbowed her twin. "Did you tell her what we found out about him?"

Her eyes shining and a smile spreading across her face, Bianca said, "Austin Tate is really Austin Gage Tate."

Fiona shrugged. "So?"

Britney marched past Fiona to the kitchen and came back with the previous day's newspaper. "He usually goes by Gage. He's Gage Tate, the billionaire, and Texas's most eligible bachelor."

GAGE CIRCLED Temptation's little airport, scanning for the limousine he'd sent to collect Fiona. When he spotted it, he didn't see her standing beside it. His heart in his throat, he landed the jet on the short landing strip, shut down the engines and climbed out.

Joe stepped out of the vehicle, nodded Gage's direction and opened the back door.

Fiona stepped out, empty-handed.

Gage frowned. He could have sworn he'd told her to pack a bag.

The redhead crossed her arms and stood beside the limousine until he stopped in front of her.

"Did you bring a bag?" he asked.

Her eyes narrowed. "I did, but I haven't quite decided whether or not I'm going with you."

"I thought we made a deal."

"I did. With Austin Tate." Her brows rose. "Not with Gage Tate, the billionaire."

A chill slipped across Gage's skin at the icy stare she leveled on him. "I didn't lie about who I am. My name is Austin Gage Tate."

She glared at him. "You should have been upfront about who you really are."

"What bothers you worse, that I go by both names, or that I'm loaded? Most women would have no problem with either circumstance."

"I'm not most women, and I don't like being misled."

"I told you. I didn't lie."

"You lied by omission."

"What difference does it make if I'm Gage or Austin? I'm the same person."

"Because if you did it once, how can I trust you not to do it again? You could have made your money in human trafficking and covered it with your construction company." She threw her hand in the air. "For all I know, you're flying me off to your compound."

His lips tingled with the urge to smile. Rather than

laughing at her announcement, he went for gentle and contrite. "I'm not going to sell you into the sex trade. I'm sorry if I misled you with the name Austin. I like a woman to get to know me as myself, not as my bank account."

Her brows furrowed. "I don't give a damn about your bank account."

"Are you coming with me or not? We need to leave if we're going to get there before dark."

"That's another thing. When you said we'd be going to a friend's ranch, I assumed a drive out into the country. Are we leaving the country?"

Gage's lips quirked on the corners. "Not the country. The state."

Fiona shook her head. "Joe, take me home." She started to climb back into the vehicle.

Seeing his hopes of avoiding Priscilla leaving with Fiona, Gage stepped forward. "Wait."

"We have nothing more to say. I won't be lied to, misled or whatever you want to call it."

"I get that. Now let me be completely honest with you. We're going to visit William Langley. His daughter will be there and I'm trying to avoid her. Langley spoils her and gives her everything she wants."

"And she wants you?"

He nodded, hating how it sounded when Fiona said it. "I want a piece of property Mr. Langley owns and I mean to buy it. The way I see it, Priscilla could make or break this deal."

Her gaze narrowed. "And you want me to run interference?" She stood with her hand on the door.

"Yes. I told him I was bringing my girlfriend. If he

and Priscilla think I'm already spoken for, it will take the focus off me and Priscilla and put it back on the deal."

"And the online dating system was just a ploy to get a date for this event?"

"Not for this event."

"So you never intended to find a mate through Leslie's program," she said, more of statement than a question. She shook her head. "So much for a computer program selecting perfect matches. I didn't buy it either."

"Maybe this will help you decide." Gage took another step forward and reached for her hand, laying ten one-hundred dollars bills in her palm.

She stared down at the money and curled her fist around it. "If I didn't need the money, I'd go home and forget I ever met Austin Gage Tate. But I can't." She stared hard at him, her eyes narrowed. "But this is strictly business, or I walk."

"Agreed. However, if you're coming as my girlfriend, we have to make it convincing."

Her lips pressed into a thin line. "I'm not sure I like the sound of that. Please specify what you think is convincing?"

"Holding hands in public, an occasional kiss to make it look real."

Before he finished talking, Fiona shook her head. "No kissing."

"Not even a peck on the cheek? How am I going to convince Priscilla you're my girlfriend if we only hold hands?"

"That's your problem. I'll go. You can call me your

girlfriend, but I'm not having sex with you, and we're not kissing."

Gage was beginning to think he should have hired an escort service. At least an escort would know how to be a fake girlfriend. He didn't have time to change lanes now. Besides which, he liked pushing Fiona's buttons and would find her more interesting than a stranger. "Deal. Only hand-holding, no sex or kissing, unless you want it."

"And I won't," she assured him, jamming the hundreds into her jeans pocket. Then she leaned into the backseat of the car and retrieved a bright pink shopping bag she had to have gotten from a lingerie shop and looped it over her arm. "All right, let's do this."

Gage glanced around her to the inside of the vehicle, looking for the rest of her things. "That's all you brought? Most women bring a fully loaded suitcase for an overnight stay."

She handed him the pink bag. "I keep telling you—and you're not getting it—I'm not most women."

He grinned. "I'm beginning to get the picture." Gage stowed her bag behind the pilot's seat, handed her up into the plane and steered her toward the co-pilot's seat.

Fiona's eyes widened and she glanced around. "Where's the pilot?"

With a wink he settled into his seat. "You're looking at him."

"You can fly this?"

"I got it here all by myself," he said with just a little sarcasm.

His announcement did nothing to ease the worried look in her eyes. "How long have you been flying?"

"Ten years. I've logged over three thousand hours flying, half of those in this plane."

She sat back, her brows still furrowed. "I don't know. What if something happens to you? I don't know how to fly a plane."

"Nothing will happen to me. If it makes you feel any better, I'll give you basic instructions as we take off and land."

He leaned over and buckled her into the safety harness, his knuckles brushing against her sides and belly as he adjusted the straps. Then he settled a headset over her ears, powered on the engines and set the plane in motion, rolling down the narrow runway. "Ready?" he said into his microphone.

Fiona shook her head. "Not really." Her fingers dug into the armrests and she stared straight ahead as the plane picked up speed. "Where are we going?"

"Colorado."

"Colorado!"

The wheels left the ground and the plane lifted into the air. Gage sighed, releasing the tension from his body. Thankfully, it was too late for Fiona to change her mind.

CHAPTER 9

An SUV was waiting at the end of the runway on William Langley's ranch in the beautiful Colorado Rockies near Leadville.

Fiona couldn't deny her excitement. She'd barely been out of Texas in all of her twenty-four years. Colorado had been on her wish list since she'd first seen pictures of the snow-covered mountains in the National Geographic magazines she'd read in the library at school. Having grown up near Temptation, Texas and gone to college in Lubbock, mountains weren't something she saw every day, or every year, for that matter.

Gage handled the aircraft with skill, maneuvering through the mountains to land it with ease on Langley's private runway.

Fiona had slept the first hour, exhausted from her sleepless night cleaning up after the busted hot water heater. But once they came within sight of the mountains, she'd woken up and stayed awake, asking so many questions, she was certain Gage would wish he'd gone stag.

The drive from the landing strip to the stately mansion perched on the side of a hill wound through hills covered in aspens and evergreens. As they neared Langley's country retreat, Fiona's mouth dropped open and her heart fluttered. "It's beautiful."

The structure was made of stone and cedar, with huge windows overlooking the mountains and valleys. A tent was set up in front of the house and master grills were smoking in the clear mountain air.

Gage climbed out first and extended a hand to her.

She let him pull her to her feet. That electric jolt powered through her where their hands connected. Even after she stood on firm ground, he didn't release her.

An older man with a shock of white hair stepped away from a group and met them halfway across the yard. "Gage, glad you could make it."

Gage—Fiona had to remind herself that everyone would refer to him as Gage, not Austin. It still rankled that he'd hidden his true identity from her when he'd shown up as her match from Leslie's system.

"Mr. Langley, this is my girlfriend, Fiona McKenzie."

She smiled. "Nice to meet you, Mr. Langley."

The older man took her hand in both of his and raised it to his lips. "The pleasure is mine." Then he pressed a brief kiss to her skin.

"Gage, darling. I was beginning to think you'd never get here." A beautiful woman dressed in neatly pressed, designer jeans, flowing white blouse and leather boots that most likely cost more than Fiona's broken-down car. Her long, luxurious, ebony hair was pulled back from her forehead and fell in sleek, straight strands that hung halfway down her back.

She hooked her arm through Gage's and pressed her full breasts against him. She barely glanced at Fiona, her nose tilting upward instead. "Come, there's someone here you'll want to say hello to."

The hairs on the back of Fiona's neck rose and her fingers curled into fists. She had the sudden urged to sink her nails into the woman face. The visceral reaction shocked Fiona. She'd never felt quite so much animosity toward any one person and it seemed to stem from the way the woman hung on Gage's body.

"Priscilla, honey, don't be rude to our guest," Mr. Langley said.

Gage untangled Priscilla's arm from his and turned to take Fiona's hand. "Priscilla, this is my girlfriend, Fiona McKenzie."

For a brief second Priscilla's eyes narrowed, and then she smiled. "Of course she's your girlfriend." The dark-haired woman gave her another raking glance. "I don't recall meeting you anywhere."

The underlying words Fiona got out of that statement was: *And what rock did you crawl out from under?* Again, her hackles rose and she fought the urge to slap the snot out of the woman. But one glance at Priscilla's father made Fiona clamp down hard on her tongue. The man loved his daughter, even if the young woman was a first-class bitch.

"Bring your little girlfriend with you." Priscilla led the way across the beautifully manicured lawn to a group of men standing beside the grills. She touched the arm of one of the men who was talking the most and cut in. "Raymond, be a dear and fetch me a mimosa from the bar."

The man smiled at her and left to get that drink.

Fiona shook her head as her gaze followed the man who'd jumped to do the woman's bidding.

Priscilla stepped into the middle of the group and smiled. "You all have had James long enough. You must share him with the rest of us." She hooked a man's elbow and led him to the edge of the group. "James Wyatt, this is Gage Tate, the man I told you about."

Wyatt held out his hand. "Tate, I've heard good things about you. When are you coming to New York City? I have a project I'd like you to consider."

Gage's eyes lit up and he fell into a deep conversation with James, dropping his hold on Fiona's hand to talk and gesture with both of his hands. Priscilla joined into their conversation. After several minutes, listening to the two men and Priscilla discussing projects and the names of buildings in Dallas, Chicago, New York City and Atlanta, Fiona lost interest and wandered to the edge of the lawn where the hillside dropped steeply down a rocky slope.

"I take it you're not as passionate about building projects as Gage?"

The role of girlfriend to a billionaire was as foreign to Fiona as swimming with crocodiles. Especially a billionaire she'd only met the day before. She didn't know anything about Gage and what he'd done to build his fortune. Fiona took the easy way out and shrugged. "I'll let them talk business. I didn't want to miss the spectacular view."

"Have you been to Colorado much?" Mr. Langley asked.

"This would be my first time."

Langley's brows rose. "Well then, you'll have to come back when you have more time. There are so many things to do and see in the state, though I love to come out here and just relax." He nodded toward his daughter. "The party was Priscilla's idea."

"Thank you for inviting us."

"Can I offer you a drink?" the older man asked.

"If there's a light beer, I'd love one." She'd really rather have more than one to loosen her up and make her feel a little less awkward among the rich. In her faded blue jeans and off-the-rack light blue blouse and scuffed cowboy boots, she felt like the poor relation at a family reunion. Tolerated, but not necessarily desired.

When Langley returned, he handed her a bottle of Guinness. "Is this all right? If not, I could get anything you'd like better."

"This is perfect. Thank you." She accepted the beer and tipped it back for a long swallow.

"If you're interested in watching, some of the gentlemen are setting up skeet shooting behind the house.

"I'd like that. My father took me hunting when I was younger." He'd taught her how to handle a gun and some tricks to help her shoot straight. She'd always got her target, bringing home her tag limit of venison each year. She'd have to remember to hunt this year since she'd be home for the season. If the old freezer still worked, the meat would help them through the winter months.

Men stood around the back lawn, facing the rising mountain behind the house.

Fiona had never shot skeet, but understood the concept. After several men tried their hand at it, she stepped forward.

"You want to try?" Mr. Langley asked, giving her a smile.

"Yes, sir."

The ranch owner nodded toward one of the men holding a gun. "Bruce, let the little lady take a turn."

The man handed her the gun and moved several feet behind where Fiona and Langley stood.

Fiona snorted. The man must think the little lady might shoot wild.

"Ready?" William asked.

Fiona weighed the shotgun in her hands and lifted it to her shoulder, sighting down the barrel. "Ready."

"Pull!" Langley called out.

A clay pigeon launched into the sky.

Fiona followed the clay disk's trajectory, drew in a breath and squeezed the trigger. The shell exploded out of the gun and shattered the clay pigeon.

The men around her cheered and another pigeon launched into the air. For the next six rounds, Fiona nailed each clay disk. When she ran out of shells, she handed the gun back to the man who'd originally been shooting.

"You were amazing," Langley said.

"Yes. Amazing," a warm voice breathed into her ear and hands circled her waist pulling her back against him. "I lost you for a while there."

Fiona's first instinct was to stiffen. With Langley

watching, she had to maintain her charade as Gage's girl and she forced herself to relax and smile. "I can entertain myself."

"I see that." He pressed a kiss to the top of her hair.

"Speaking of entertainment," Langley said, "I have a stable full of horses that need exercise, if you'd care to ride."

Fiona's heart thrilled at the prospect. She loved to ride and, on a horse, she wouldn't be expected to carry on a conversation with other guests. "I love to ride."

"Thought you might," Gage murmured.

She stared at him. "Why?"

"You live on a ranch." He winked. "And your dossier indicated a love of horses and riding."

Fiona snorted softly. "Bianca and Britney."

"So far your sisters have been spot on."

"Remind me to thank them. I think."

Gage handed the shotgun to a nearby assistant and pulled her into his arms. "Here comes Priscilla. Play like you like me a little."

Fiona wrapped her arms around his middle and laid her cheek to his chest. The subtle scent of his cologne and the heady maleness of the man made it easy to remain pressed to him for longer than was necessary.

"There you are." Langley's daughter converged on them, her color heightened, her eyes narrowing at Fiona. "We're going for a ride. I have the perfect horse picked out for you, Gage."

"And for Fiona?" he asked, his brows rising.

"Does she ride?" Priscilla asked, her nose tilting higher.

Fiona turned to Priscilla, her lips curving into a smile. "She does."

Priscilla touched a finger to her chin. "I might know of a horse that would suit her."

At the calculating look in the other woman's eye, Fiona guessed the horse would be either an old nag or the wildest horse in the barn. Either way, Fiona could handle it. She was good with horses, even the slow ones, and enjoyed a challenge. Riding in the Colorado Rockies made it even better. "Perfect. Let's ride."

Glad she'd worn her comfortable jeans and cowboy boots, she left her arm around Gage's lean waist as they followed Priscilla to the stables behind the huge house.

Ranch hands had the horses saddled and ready for anyone wishing to ride.

Priscilla led them to a big, beautiful black stallion that had to be over sixteen hands high. "Gage, I thought you might like Blaze."

He nodded. "And for Fiona?"

Priscilla pointed to a small sorrel mare that appeared dwarfed next to the stallion. She stood patiently to the side. "Mabel was my mother's horse. She's a little older, but still has a lot of life left in her."

The graying at her nose gave the horse's age away. Fiona guessed she was close to twenty years old, but she appeared in good health and well taken care of. "She's beautiful," Fiona stated.

Gage gathered the reins for Blaze and Mabel and led them out of the stable.

Priscilla led a stunning bay mare with a highly polished saddle out into the open and mounted gracefully.

"Need a hand?" Gage asked.

Fiona smiled up at him. "Thank you, but I can manage." She adjusted the stirrups to fit her legs and swung up in the saddle.

Gage mounted the stallion. The animal pranced in a circle eager to be off.

Fiona reined her mare around, patted her neck and studied Gage as he easily brought his animal under control. He'd obviously ridden a horse before. Now that she was his "girlfriend", Fiona wished she had the advantage of reading over his dossier from Leslie's dating service. She wondered what else they might have in common.

Six riders left the yard, climbing up a mountain trail, weaving in and out of tall pines. The pace was steady and measured, the trail narrowing in some places with steep drop-offs.

Mabel seemed to know the path well enough and was agile despite her age.

Fiona let the horse do the work and took the opportunity to enjoy the incredible scenery between stands of trees.

At the top of a rise the trail opened out on a high mountain meadow filled with columbine flowers and lush green grass.

"I'll race you to the creek on the other side of the pass!" Priscilla jabbed her heels into her horse's flanks. The animal leaped forward and charged across the field.

Gage's stallion whinnied and reared, desperate to follow. For a moment Gage held his reins tight, his gaze flashing to Fiona.

"Go on," she said, as if Gage needed permission.

The stallion reared again and Gage gave him his head. The horse shot out across the meadow, his long, beautiful legs eating the distance between him and the mare in the lead. Gage leaned over the horse's neck, completely at ease in the saddle.

Fiona's chest swelled with feelings she hadn't experienced before. Pride for a person she was pretending to be in love with. But more than that, a flood of desire washed over her for the gorgeous man, riding the stallion like he'd been born to it.

Mabel trotted out into the field and stopped to munch on the grass.

The two riders racing ahead disappeared around a rocky escarpment.

Fiona gave Mabel a moment or two with the grass, then pulled back on the reins and nudged the horse forward. As they neared the overhang, a horse appeared, riderless.

For a horrifying moment, Fiona thought it was the stallion, but as it passed, she could see the sleek red of the bay mare's body as she raced for home.

"Come on Mabel, let's see what happened." Fiona urged the horse into a gallop, hurrying around the edge of the rocky outcropping. The trail dipped into a narrow valley crowded with trees.

Her pulse speeding, Fiona wondered if Priscilla and Gage had been thrown. Horses hooves pounded behind her as the others followed her.

Mabel slowed to pick her way down the hill, carefully placing her hooves on the loose gravel. When the path leveled, they passed through a stand of trees. Ahead, Fiona spotted the black stallion standing by a creek. The stallion dropped his head to drink the cool, clear water.

As the animal shifted to the left, he revealed Gage holding Priscilla in his arms.

A flash of something white-hot speared through Fiona. Gage was her man. What was Priscilla doing in his arms? Then she had to remind herself Gage wasn't really hers. Then again, he'd asked her to run interference between him and Priscilla.

Mabel trotted toward the stallion and came to a sedate halt. Fiona raised her brows. "Should I be worried something's going on between the two of you?" Though her teeth grated, she forced the words to sound nonchalant, as if she didn't have a worry in the world about Gage's fidelity. She swung down from her mount and stood beside the pair.

Priscilla laughed and clung to Gage.

Gage's lips pressed into a thin line. "Priscilla seems to have lost her horse."

"The silly mare spooked at a marmot while I was dismounting. My foot caught in the stirrup. The next thing I knew, I was on the ground. Gage was kind enough to help me up." She curled her arm around his neck and pouted. "Now my mount is well on her way home. I suppose I'll have to ride back with someone."

"That won't be necessary." Gage lifted Priscilla's arm from around his neck and stepped away. "You can ride Mabel. Fiona can ride back with me on Blaze."

"But—"

Gage ignored the woman and swung up on Blaze. He held out his hand to Fiona. "Coming, darlin'?"

Fiona handed Priscilla Mabel's reins. "She's a lovely

horse. Thank you for allowing me to ride her." Then she laid her hand in Gage's, placed her foot on his in the stirrup and let him swing her up behind him. She wrapped her arms around his waist and smiled down at the disgruntled look on Priscilla's face. "Mmmm, this is much nicer."

Gage tipped his cowboy hat. "See you back at the stables."

"Aren't you going to wait for me?"

Gage nodded toward the other members of the riding party as they trotted to a halt beside Mabel. "I'm sure there are plenty of others who'd be more than happy to help."

Gage nudged the stallion into a gentle lope, headed back the way they'd come. As they crossed over the field, he slowed the horse to a walk, his chest shaking.

"Are you okay?" Fiona asked.

The shaking continued and then Gage laughed out loud. "She turned her horse loose. I saw her slap the mare's ass."

"She didn't fall?" Fiona loosened her hold around Gage's middle. Her own funny bone tickled, she giggled, then chortled and finally her laughter joined his.

Startled, the stallion leaped forward and took off at a gallop.

Fiona grabbed Gage's middle and held on tight, loving the feel of pressing her face against his muscular back as they followed the trail back to the stable.

When they arrived, Gage eased her to the ground and dismounted. Ranch hands waited nearby to take the horse.

"Thanks, but we can take care of him."

Fiona tossed the stirrup over the saddle and loosened the girth.

Gage leaned close to her ear. "Let the ranch hands do it."

"But we're perfectly capable," she said.

"It's their job, and you don't want to put them out of work, do you?"

Her hand stilled on the leather strap. When he put it that way, it made more sense. "Oh. Well, then." She backed away from the horse. "Thank you," she said and turned with Gage. "I've never gone riding where I didn't take care of my own horse," she said as they left the barn.

"I know. I feel the same. But sometimes you have to let others do the work they're being paid to do. Come on, let's find our rooms and get cleaned up for the barbeque."

Though the scenery was stunning and the mountain air crisp and so clean she could fill her lungs to capacity, Fiona never felt more out of place. She worked for a living and worked to live. No one brushed her horses or mucked her stalls. She had always been the one to jump in and help, from stringing fences to repairing the roof on the barn. Having someone else do the things she normally did made her feel...useless.

"Is this what it's like to be rich?" she asked.

"How's that?"

"Like you can't do anything for yourself?"

"Sometimes. But when you have a lot of money, others depend on you to keep it coming. You employ people to do the things you no longer have time to do. It frees you up to move on to more important tasks."

Fiona held his hand as they walked toward the house. "I guess it all boils down to what tasks you consider more important."

Before Gage could reply to her comment, they'd entered the house and were met by one of the maids. "Mr. Tate, Ms. McKenzie, I'm Rosa, your maid. Your bags were taken to your room. If you follow me, I'll show you where that is."

Gage had to commend Langley's staff on being one step ahead. Knowing their names before Gage had been introduced to the maid meant someone had clued them in on who was who at the Langley party.

The maid led them up an elegantly curved staircase to the second floor, making a right at the top of the stairs. They traversed a long, wide hallway decorated with beautiful paintings of the surrounding mountains and alpine meadows.

Rosa entered one of the rooms and held the door open for Gage and Fiona. "This will be your suite for the evening." She crossed the room and opened a door at the far side. "You have your own private bath. There are additional towels in the cabinet and toiletries. If you should need anything else, don't hesitate to ask." The maid turned and left, pulling the door closed behind her.

"Uh, Gage."

Gage turned to where Fiona stood in the middle of the bedroom, staring at the king-sized bed taking up center-stage in the spacious suite. He fought a smile at the way her brows furrowed and she chewed on her lower lip. "Is something wrong with the room?" he asked, knowing exactly what met with her objection.

"There's only one bed."

"Langley must have assumed we're sleeping together."

"Well disavow him of the presumption."

"If I do that, Priscilla might slip into my room at night, placing me in an awkward situation where her father is concerned. I don't intend to give the man reason to stand guard at a shotgun wedding for his darling daughter."

Fiona's frown deepened. "She'd do that?"

"You saw how she tried to manipulate me into riding double with her earlier. I wouldn't put anything past that woman."

"Why is she so dead set on having you?"

Gage held out his arms. "Well, look at me. What's not to love?"

Fiona rolled her eyes. "You're arrogant and pushy."

"Priscilla sees those as attributes and she doesn't let little things like that bother her."

"You two are perfect or each other."

"Hardly." Gage shoved a hand through his hair. "Ever since my photo was plastered over the cover of the Dallas Journal as the most eligible bachelor, she's been after me."

"You poor baby." Fiona patted his cheek, her expression deadpan, not at all empathetic to his plight. "That still doesn't solve the issue of only one bed in this room." She turned and pointed to a loveseat situated near a picture window overlooking the valley below. "You'll have to sleep there."

"Why? The bed is plenty big enough for both of us."

She crossed her arms. "What part of no sex did you not understand? We made a deal."

Gage held up his hands. "Okay, okay. I'll sleep all cramped up on a little bitty couch, while you sleep on the luxurious king-sized bed."

"I will." She pulled the elastic band from where it secured her ponytail, letting her hair fall loose around her shoulders. Then she gathered the pink bag and headed for the bathroom. "In the meantime, I'm first in the shower."

Gage stared at the door long after Fiona closed it between them. The woman was stubborn, and mouthy...and beautiful when her green eyes flashed with her auburn hair framing her face. The lingering warmth where her arms had wrapped around his middle on the ride back to the house and the memory of her laughter echoed in his thoughts. Gage wanted to hear her laughter again, it was so free and joyous, something he hadn't felt in years. With the pressures of his businesses, the press and social commitments, he'd long since stopped having fun. Riding with Fiona today reminded him of some of the simpler joys in life. If he wasn't careful, his hired girlfriend might be more of a threat to him than Priscilla. She might make him want more than a temporary girlfriend. She might make him want what members of the Billionaires Anonymous Club had been trying to tell him. A home, family, someone to share his successes as well as his burdens.

Gage shook his head. No. Fiona was only there for the money. Otherwise, she would have nothing to do with him.

He stepped out on the balcony, oblivious to the beauty of his surroundings, his thoughts drifting back to the woman in the shower, on the other side of a single wall. She'd be naked, the water dripping over her breasts and lower.

Gage groaned. No sex.

He'd be hard pressed to keep his hands to himself. The woman had a body that tempted the saint out of him. Oh, who was he kidding? He didn't have a saint in him. Or so his image consultant would have him believe.

"The bathroom is yours," a soft voice called out.

He turned to see her standing barefooted in a flowing mint-green dress that draped her curves to perfection, the hem stopping mid-thigh. Her hair hung down her back, damp and curling. She'd applied a little eye makeup that emphasized her beautiful green eyes.

Gage almost reached out to take her into his arms, remembering before he embarrassed himself that he'd promised not to make love to her. "I'll be ready in ten minutes." He walked past her and into the shower before his body took over from his head and he broke his promise.

Ten minutes under a cold shower wouldn't be nearly long enough.

CHAPTER 10

THE BARBEQUE WAS FANCIER than any Fiona had ever attended—catered by a chef renowned nationwide for his excellent barbeque skills. Elaborate grills had been imported and arranged on the edges of the lawn. Tables had been placed around a huge, stone fire pit with a fire blazing in the center to chase away the high country chill.

The food was excellent and the company was entertaining, but there was something missing. Any barbeque Fiona had attended in the past included family and friends, a sense of community where a person could relax and be herself.

Throughout the meal, Fiona picked at the fabulous food and counted the minutes until they could go back to their room and fight over who got the bed. Her belly warmed, heat spreading throughout her body and pooling low. The man was far too attractive. She could forget about actually sleeping when every move he made would inspire sexy thoughts.

Hell, she hadn't even considered what he might sleep in. Her cheeks heated and her heart pounded against her ribs. What if he slept in the nude?

Heaven help me.

When the food and dishes had been cleared away, a band played country music on the patio, inviting guests to dance in the twinkle lights strategically placed all over the trees and blossoming bushes.

"Would you like to dance?" Gage extended a hand.

Fiona stared at the hand and shook her head, afraid if she took it, he'd feel her clammy palm and ask why she was so hot. She'd have to come up with a lie to cover the fact she'd been thinking of him lying naked on that ridiculously small loveseat. Swallowing hard to quell her errant thoughts, she answered, "I don't feel like dancing."

"What's wrong?"

She shrugged and stared at the fire pit. "I guess I miss my family." It was true. She hadn't been home long before she flew off to Colorado to play the part of Gage Tate's girlfriend.

"You were away at school for a long time. You miss them after only one day away?"

With a sigh, she looked up at him. It was much easier talking about her family than the mixed up sensations she was feeling. "I missed them the entire time I was gone, and went home whenever I could afford to put gas in my car and take the time off work."

"They mean a lot to you," he said.

"They do. Ever since my mother died, not a day goes by that I don't think about them. You never know how much time you have with your family until one of them passes away."

Gage stared into the darkness.

"What about you?" she asked, shifting her gaze from the fire to Gage. "Where is your family?"

Gage shrugged. "I don't know."

Fiona frowned. "What do you mean, you don't know?"

"I was left at a church when I was four. From that point on, I was passed around from one foster family to another until I was old enough to go out on my own."

Fiona's heart ached for the little boy abandoned by his parents. "Didn't you form any lasting connections with any of your foster families?"

"Only my last foster family. They were old, but they encouraged me to play sports. I was pretty good at football and earned a scholarship to Texas A&M. I played football and worked when I could to put myself through school."

"And look at you now. You made it." She smiled. When he didn't return the smile, hers faded. "What happed to your foster family?"

"They died in a wreck. A drunk driver hit them head on." Gage glanced her way, his blue eyes dark pools of pain. "They were on their way home from watching one of my football games."

She touched his arm. "I'm sorry for your loss."

"It was a long time ago."

"They never got to see how successful you became."

He shrugged and responded in a low tone, "It didn't matter."

"What about women? Have you been married, engaged, in love?"

His jaw hardened and he again glanced away.

Fiona held her breath and waited for his response. She began to think he wouldn't answer.

When Fiona gave up and cast about for the next topic, Gage said, "I was engaged once."

Fiona's heart stopped. She could imagine a woman like Priscilla with stunning black hair, perfect makeup, all the right clothes on a flawless figure and able to hold her own in the company of mega-millionaires. Lead sank to the pit of her belly. Fiona would never fit into Gage's world. She wore jeans of a generic brand. "What happened?" she asked, fully expecting to hear he'd dropped the woman.

He shrugged. "She got a better offer."

Fiona blinked. "Better offer? Was she crazy?"

He smiled. "Thanks. But it was before I made my first billion. I was sinking every cent I had into building my business, not spending it on her."

Fiona nodded. "You have to invest money to make money, right?" Then she giggled.

Gage shot a narrowed glance her way. "What's so funny?"

"I don't know." Her giggles turned to chuckles and an embarrassing snort.

Gage glared at her. "I fail to see the humor in being dumped."

"I'm sorry." She wiped tears from her eyes. "I had a flashback of Priscilla standing beside Mabel as we rode off on Blaze." She giggled again and clapped a hand over her mouth. When she had control again, she looked at him. "As far as I see it, you dodged a bullet with your ex-fiancée." She grabbed his hand. "How about we dodge another? Priscilla is on her way over, I suspect to ask you to dance."

Gage resisted for only a second. One glance toward the advancing Ms. Langley and he was on his feet, half-dragging Fiona toward the band.

The band was playing a lively song perfect for a two-step. Gage pulled Fiona into his arms and stepped out with confidence, leading her through the steps until she followed him perfectly. She was laughing and breathless by the time the song ended and slowed into a belly-rubbing love song.

Gage tugged her against his chest. She didn't fight him, blaming the chill night air on her need to be close to him. She laid her cheek against his neck, inhaling that heady combination of cologne and Gage, a scent she'd forever associate with him. Long after this weekend was over and she returned home. For now she only had to think about the moon and stars shining down over the Rockies and the man holding her in his arms like he really cared.

Too bad it was all a ruse. She'd wake up the next morning to reality. Tonight she could dream.

As the music ended, the band thanked the audience for inviting them to play. Some of the guests had already retired to their rooms.

"I guess that's our cue." Fiona looked up into Gage's eyes, her heart thrumming against her ribs. "I'm going to turn in."

He kissed the top of her head. "You do that. I'll be up

in a few minutes to give you time to yourself in the bathroom."

A little disappointed that he wasn't coming up with her, Fiona nodded and left, entering the house alone. When she stepped through the door, she paused and glanced back. Priscilla had chosen the opportunity to capture Gage's arm.

"He's a grown man," Fiona muttered. "He can handle it."

"Ah, Ms. McKenzie." William Langley appeared beside her, carrying a crystal glass filled with amber liquid. "I trust you enjoyed the barbeque?"

"Yes, sir. I did." She smiled at the older man, sensing a good heart in the gentleman. Too bad his daughter wasn't more like him. "Thank you for inviting us to your lovely home."

"You're more than welcome." He tipped his head toward Gage. "I have to admit, I wasn't happy to hear Mr. Tate had a girlfriend. I had hoped he and Priscilla would get together."

Fiona swallowed hard to keep from gasping at the man's bluntness. "I'd like to say I'm sorry, but I'm glad it didn't work out for Gage and Priscilla."

Langley chuckled. "Don't take it wrong. You and Gage are perfect for each other. He and Priscilla would never have worked out. But you can't fault a father for wanting the best for his little girl."

Fiona's cheeks heated. "Thank you." Apparently the charade they'd put on for the Langleys had done its job. At least on Mr. Langley's end. She was happy for Gage, but she didn't like lying to Mr. Langley, who had turned out to be a nice man.

The older man patted her hand and leaned over to hug her briefly. "Don't let me keep you from turning in. In the meantime, I'll rescue Mr. Tate from my daughter's clutches. She can be a first class bitch, but I love her."

Fiona blinked. Had the man just called his own daughter a bitch? She didn't wait around to witness Mr. Langley rescuing Gage from Priscilla. She climbed the sweeping staircase to the second floor and entered the room she and Gage would share for the night. She changed into the long Texas Tech T-shirt she used as a night gown, brushed her teeth and stood for a moment in the bedroom, staring at the king-sized bed, wondering what it would be like to lie naked with Gage, how it would feel to be skin to skin, making love with the gorgeous billionaire.

Like a dream she'd wake up from with a whole lot of regret.

Fiona grabbed a blanket and settled on the loveseat. The drapes remained open to the night sky. She lay beneath the blanket, staring out at the silhouette of the mountains, listening for the sound of footsteps in the hallway. After a half hour passed, the sleepless night before took its toll and she gave up the fight to stay awake, drifting into a dream where wishes came true.

GAGE STAYED up late into the night talking with William Langley after Priscilla finally got bored of the men rehashing ideas they had for downtown Dallas. They ended up in Langley's study talking over glasses of iced tea, instead of the fine whiskey William had offered.

Gage insisted he had to fly back to Texas the following day and needed a clear head.

Near midnight, Langley still hadn't committed to the sale of the property.

Gage hadn't complained or tried to end the conversation earlier, knowing that if he went back to the room he'd share with Fiona, he'd be hard-pressed to keep his hands off the pretty redhead. However the longer he was away from her, the more he wanted to be with her. Her smile, laughter and her grasp of what was important made him feel strangely at peace at the same time as her body wound his up on knots.

"I like you, Tate," William said, walking him to the door of the study. "I've a good mind to sell that property to you."

"I can't say I'd be disappointed."

"I like you and that pretty little redhead you brought with you. You two remind me of my wife and me back before we had two nickels to rub together. Don't let that girl go. She's a keeper."

Gage nodded, unsure of how to respond when his dealings with Fiona might only last until he took her back to her home in Texas. After that, she probably wouldn't have anything to do with him.

"Thank you for your hospitality, Mr. Langley."

"Call me William."

"Good night, William." He shook hands with the man and left him in the foyer.

Now that he was on his way back to the room he shared with Fiona, he couldn't wait to get there. More than likely she'd given up and gone to sleep. That would be okay too. Then he could watch her without her throwing something.

With a deep sigh, he pushed through the door of their assigned bedroom only to find a light shining on the nightstand and an empty bed.

A momentary panic filled him as he scanned the room, his gaze landing on the loveseat near the window. Curled up in a blanket, her hand tucked under her cheek and her auburn hair in wild disarray around her, lay Fiona, sound asleep, her long legs pulled up against her chest to fit the sofa.

Warmth seeped into Gage's chest. Not just the warmth of desire, but something else he'd never felt for a woman. Not even his ex-fiancée, Lacy. This woman loved her family and would do anything for them. Gage's foster parents had been the same and had included him as part of their family. When they'd died, he'd stopped caring, except for the small group of friends he belonged to, all committed to making more of their lives than what they'd started with.

Gage scooped Fiona into his arms.

She stirred, blinked her eyes open and smiled at him with soft, kissable lips. "Hey."

"Hey, you. Go back to sleep."

"With you?" she murmured, sliding an arm around his neck and pressing a braless breast against his chest.

Gage sucked in a steadying breath as he carried her across the room to the bed. "No," he said. He should have felt good about resisting the temptation of Fiona, but all he could think of was how much he wanted to kiss her and slide his hands beneath the shirt.

As it was, Fiona's T-shirt rode up on her thighs,

exposing a lot more of her legs than he'd seen thus far. They were tight, athletic and warm against his hands.

Yeah, it was going to be a long night.

As he laid her on the sheets, she hooked her hands behind his neck and refused to let go, forcing him to lean over her.

"You need to go back to sleep," he said, through gritted teeth, fighting the urge to crawl in bed beside the tempting witch.

"Just one kiss," she whispered.

"You don't know what you're asking."

"Yes, I do."

"You're still half asleep. You won't remember it in the morning."

Fiona stared up into his eyes, her own green ones clear and focused. "I'm not asleep. Just one kiss and I'll let you go." Her brows pulled together. "Unless you don't want to kiss me."

"Far from it. I'm trying to be a gentleman."

"Being a gentleman is highly overrated."

"Not according to my image consultant."

Fiona released her hold on his neck and cupped his cheeks between her palms. "I think your image is pretty damned sexy."

Gage shook his head. "I promised I wouldn't make love to you."

"Unless I asked," she finished. "I'm asking. Please just one kiss."

"That's the problem, darlin'. I won't be able to stop at just a kiss. If you want a kiss, you'll have to risk taking on a lot more than that."

Fiona's gaze remained steady, refusing to drift away

from his. With every breath she took, her breasts rose beneath the faded cotton of her T-shirt. "I'll take whatever you have to offer."

"This wasn't part of the bargain," he said, his resolve crumbling.

"I know." Fiona drew him down to her until his lips hovered over hers.

"You won't regret it later?" he murmured, caught up in the sexy droop of her eyelids.

She shook her head.

His eyes narrowed. "I'm not making any commitments just because I make love to you."

"I'm not asking for any. And if you don't kiss me already, I might change my mind."

Gage sealed his mouth over hers, plundering the lips he'd been dreaming about throughout his discussion with Langley.

Fiona opened to him, allowing his tongue to slide between her teeth and claim hers in a long, wet glide, while he slipped a hand beneath her shirt.

She arched her back, pressing her breast into his palm, a low moan rising up from her chest to escape with a sigh into his mouth.

Gage's groin tightened as he squeezed the rounded swell and pinched the tip of her nipple, rolling the bud between his thumb and forefinger. "Just say no and I'll stop here," he said, praying she wouldn't.

Fiona sat up and brushed a hand through his hair, then reached for the buttons on his shirt. "You and I are from different worlds."

"Not really," he started, his body stiff with the effort to control himself.

Fiona pressed a finger to his lips and he kissed it.

"After today, the mountains, the dancing...the kiss..." she sighed, her breath warming his belly. "What I'm telling you is that I'm not asking for tomorrow. I don't want anything from you but tonight." She threw open his shirt and brushed her fingertips across his abs, her brows rising in challenge. "So what do you say?"

"I don't know, yee-haw seems inadequate, but the only thing I can think of with you touching me like that."

Fiona's lips parted in a smile. "I'd settle for yee-haw."

Needing no more of an invitation, he yanked his shirt off and threw it across the room.

Fiona reached for the button on his trousers and slipped it loose, her fingers capturing the zipper tab and dragging it downward. She caught the waistband of his pants in her hands and pushed them down his hips. Her gaze rose to his as his cock sprang free.

"Commando?" She chuckled as she pushed the trousers downward.

"Damn right." God, she was sexy in the oversized T-shirt, her hair rumpled from sleep. Gage threaded his fingers through her curls and bent to capture her lips. He toed off his shoes and stepped free of them and his trousers all in the length of one beautiful kiss.

When he broke for air, he reached for the hem of her shirt and eased it up her body, slowly like unwrapping a special present. His gaze followed the fabric over flat abs, up her torso to the luscious swells of her breasts. Temptation took hold and he ripped the shirt over her head flinging it across the bed.

On a mission to get her naked, he slipped his fingers

into the waistband of her shorts and panties and dragged them down her legs.

Fiona sat up, spreading her legs wide enough he could step between. "I've never been this exposed to a man before."

"Never?"

She glanced up at him with a twisted smile. "I'm not a virgin, it's just that having sex was something done in the dark. This..." her gaze swept the length of him, the flash of heat in her eyes setting off an answering firestorm in his belly, "...is so much better." Her voice dropped into a gravelly murmur.

Gage's cock jerked to attention, jutting out on level with her lips. He wouldn't ask, but if she took him with her mouth...Sweet Jesus, he'd come apart.

"I like seeing what I'm getting." She rested her hands on his hip, sliding them down his thighs and back up. "I've been imagining what it would feel like to touch your skin like this." Again her hands coursed over his hips and thighs, teasing him, tempting him, making him so hard he could drive nails with his dick.

"Do you have any idea what you're doing to me?" he said, his voice raspy and tight.

She shifted her hand, cutting across his groin to curl it around his cock. "Oh, I think it's pretty obvious." Then she leaned forward and tapped her tongue to the bulbous head.

The air hissed out of Gage's lungs and he dug his fingers into her scalp. "I don't know how much more I can take. You make me feel like a teenage boy about to blow."

She tsked her tongue. "You can't do that. Not when

we've only just started. I want to touch you all over. To taste you in my mouth and then take you inside me."

Her words were almost as seductive as her naked body, bringing him dangerously close to the edge. "So? What's stopping you?"

"I don't know what you'll like." She glanced up at him.

"Darlin' anything you do will be amazing."

"Like this?" She touched her tongue to his cock and slipped it around the rim.

Gage drew in a ragged breath. "Holy hell, yes."

Her other hand cupped his balls and rolled them between her fingers as she wrapped her lips around him and leaned forward, taking him into her mouth.

Eager for her warmth, he thrust forward.

Fiona gripped his hips and guided him in and out at a steadily increasing pace.

Gage twisted his hands in her hair and thrust to her pace, holding back to make it last as long as he could take it. When he thought he would explode, he jerked free.

Her lips wet and swollen, Fiona gazed up at him. "Not good enough?"

"Damn, woman. You're setting me on fire. It was all I could do not to come in your mouth."

"Then why did you stop?"

"I want you to be as hot as you made me." He lifted her in his arms and tossed her to the middle of the bed, climbing up between her legs like a conquering hero. He was so close to the edge, he wanted to pound his chest with his fists and shout. Now wasn't the time. Gage wanted Fiona to shoot over the top with him, to feel the same sense of excitement and release when he finally came.

He bent her knees and settled between her legs.

Fiona levered up on her elbows, her brows furrowing. "What are you doing?"

"I'm going to set your world on fire." Then he lifted her bottom with his hands, parted her folds with his thumbs and swept his tongue across her clit.

CHAPTER 11

AN EXPLOSION of sensations ricocheted through Fiona's body and she fell back against the bed, curling her fingers into the sheets. "Sweet Jesus," she gasped.

"Oh baby, you haven't seen anything yet." Again he lifted her to his mouth, teasing the nubbin of flesh with the tip of his tongue. He touched, tapped and laved her until she squirmed, her core tensing, tingles spreading from the point of his contact outward to the very tips of her fingers and toes. She dug her heels into the mattress and thrust upward, wanting more. "Please."

"Please what? Please stop?" He blew his warm breath over her heated center.

"Please," she cried. "More!"

With a deep-throated chuckle, he gave it to her, his tongue dipping into her channel and tracing a line back up to her clit. Again. And again, until she couldn't breathe, her body no longer her own, every move instinctive, primal and scorching hot.

One last flick of his tongue and she rocketed to the heavens, her fingers digging into his scalp as she cried out, "Gage!"

He didn't stop touching her intimately until her body dropped to the mattress, her muscles quivering with her release.

Gage leaned over the side of the bed, grabbed his trousers, fished his wallet from inside and pulled out a foil packet. With deft movements, he tore open the packet and rolled a ribbed condom down his cock.

Too shaken to move, Fiona lay with her knees spread wide, ready for him.

Hard as steel and fully protected, Gage kissed his way up her torso, claimed a breast with his mouth and nipped the tip lightly, then he found his way to her mouth, kissing her until she didn't care if she ever breathed again. As she wrapped her arms around his neck and kissed him back, he pressed the tip of his erection against her opening, dipping in and out to coat himself in her juices.

Fiona couldn't wait a minute longer. "I want you," she whispered, wrapped her legs around his waist and dug her heels into his buttocks, urging him to finish what he'd started.

He obliged, thrusting deeply, stretching the walls of her channel. He started slow, building up speed until he hammered in and out.

Fiona dropped her feet to the mattress and pushed up, meeting him thrust for thrust until he slammed into her one last time, burying himself to the hilt. He held there, his body tense, his cock throbbing. For the longest moment, time stood still and Fiona felt more complete than she'd ever felt in her life. She was exactly where she wanted to be and with the man who made her feel so incredible, it could only be a dream. Nothing was this magical and as mind-blowing as making love with Gage Tate.

As they slowly drifted back to earth, Gage rolled to the side, pulling her with him, maintaining the intimate connection. He wrapped his arms around her and held her close, nestled against his chest.

Fiona inhaled that special scent of Gage, his cologne, his musk and the intoxicating aroma of sex. The afterglow of their union warmed her, cocooning her in the fantasy. She refused to wake and face the reality of their true relationship. Tomorrow would be soon enough. For the time being, she wanted to bask in the alluring tenderness of Gage's embrace.

GAGE WOKE Fiona once that night to make sweet love to her again. And she woke him in the gray light of predawn, peppering hot kisses across his chest and face, drawing him out of a sensuous dream of making love to her into the reality of holding her in his arms. The dream wasn't nearly as satisfying as the reality of Fiona lying beneath him, him thrusting into her slick, tight channel. They fit together so perfectly he couldn't imagine making love to any other female for the rest of his life.

They fell into a deep sleep as dawn crept over the jagged peaks of the Rockies.

Gage woke first and spent the first few minutes of consciousness watching Fiona curled against him, her skin pale in the morning light, her hair splayed across the white pillowcase. He loved how warm and soft her body fit against his and he didn't want that moment to end.

Unfortunately the rest of the houseguests were awake and moving around, and Gage and Fiona had to fly back to Texas in a couple hours.

With a great deal of effort, Gage forced himself to slip out of the bed, grab his duffle bag, and enter the bathroom, closing the door behind him. If they weren't at Langley's house, he would have stayed in bed all day long, making sweet love to Fiona.

As he showered and dressed for the day, he went over her words from the night before. She hadn't asked for anything but the night.

He'd told her making love to her wasn't a commitment. After last night and the incredible connection he'd felt with her, he couldn't imagine letting her go. He wanted her. But would he want her after the freshness of a new relationship wore off? More importantly, would she still want him?

His mind in turmoil, one thought stood out above all else.

One night with Fiona wasn't nearly enough.

Dressed and ready to face the day, he opened the bathroom door.

Fiona stood in her T-shirt, her bag in hand, biting her bottom lip. When she saw him, she gave him a shy smile. "My turn?"

He nodded, his heart lodged in his throat, every nerve and muscle in his body screaming for him to drag her into his arms and take her back to bed. But he held back, afraid of the intensity of his reaction to seeing her.

Fiona ducked around him and entered the bathroom, closing the door between them.

If there had been a chance to hold her and kiss her, he'd missed it completely.

What was wrong with him? Somewhere deep inside, he knew what they'd had the night before was special. And it scared the crap out of him. After his fiancée dumped him for a wealthier man, he'd suffered with trust issues.

Though he knew Fiona was as true to her word as people came, he wasn't sure where this was going.

Leaning close to the door, he called out. "I'm headed down. I'll see you at breakfast."

As he left the bedroom and descended the curving staircase, he called himself every kind of coward. He'd spent the last couple of years working so hard he hadn't had time to dwell on love or anything other than the next project. And after the disappointment of Lacy, he hadn't wanted to delve into romance. Old habits were hard to break. He needed time.

THE FLIGHT back to Texas was accomplished in silence. Though she was tired, Fiona couldn't sleep, her mind going over the events of the previous night and early morning. Yes, she'd told him she didn't want a commitment, that she was only into sex with Gage for the one night, making no promises for tomorrow. But damn! He'd gone from the most amazing lover, who ensured she was as satisfied as he was, to completely ignoring her.

Fiona couldn't lie to herself. She wanted more. Yet, having laid the ground rules, she couldn't ask for it. By the time they'd landed, her stomach hurt from going over and over every word spoken in the heat of passion. Why had he shut down?

The limousine waited at the Temptation landing strip, Joe standing beside it as Gage taxied to a stop.

Fiona hurried to unclip her seat belt before Gage could release his, only the buckle hung. She fought to free it, her fingers tearing at the metal clasp. Tears filled her eyes. Swallowing hard on the sob rising up her throat, she wasn't surprised when Gage brushed her hands aside and flipped the catch open.

He exited the aircraft first and turned to help her down, holding onto her hand even after she was safely on the ground. "Thank you for coming with me."

She averted her face, hoping Gage wouldn't see the moisture pooling in her eyes. "I hope it turned out the way you wanted with Langley."

Gage nodded. "It did, and all because of you."

She stared at her hand in his, her cheeks heating at the unexpected compliment.

"I have one more favor to ask."

She glanced up, her gaze meeting his. The heat she'd seen the night before flashed in his eyes and her heart fluttered.

"There's a charity ball this Saturday. I would like for you to come with me."

Her heart lifted, butterfly wings batted at the inside

of her stomach, joy filling her chest. He was asking her out.

Fiona opened her mouth to respond, but he went on before she could.

"It would be the same deal. One thousand dollars up front, another thousand after the ball." He pulled a wad of bills out of his pocket and laid it in her hand. "That's two thousand. The rest of this weekend's pay and the down payment for the ball if you'll agree to go with me."

Gage had effectively poked a hole in the balloon of her happiness and the air leaked out, leaving her feeling deflated and depressed. Had she been the only one to feel any real connection the previous night? Or had the connection been all in her mind? It most definitely wasn't in *his* mind, if he felt he had to pay her to go out with him again.

She started to hand the money back to him, but he curled her fingers around it and stepped away. "I'll send transportation to pick you up next Saturday."

"I haven't said yes."

"I'll send for you anyway. If you come, good. If not, I'll have your answer."

"Austin—Gage, even if I did say yes, I couldn't compete with the other ladies who will be attending. The closest thing to a formal evening gown I have is my mother's old wedding dress. I can't come with you." She shoved her hand out.

"I'll come up with something."

"I won't take your charity, Gage. The McKenzies might not have a lot of money, but we don't take hand outs."

"No handouts then. Whatever I come up with will be on loan."

She frowned. "Like a rental?"

"Something like that." Gage handed her the pink bag. "Thank you again for performing your part this weekend. If you'll excuse me, I have to get back to Dallas. Joe will take you home." He turned, walked back to his airplane and climbed in.

With a hand full of money, her heart empty of emotion, Fiona walked in a daze toward the limousine, her eyes filling with tears. When she reached Joe, he wordlessly opened the door for her.

Thankful he didn't say anything, Fiona climbed into the back seat, unable to hold back the tears any longer. She glanced out the window once as the little jet taxied down the runway and took off. What had just happened?

She'd gotten what she wanted, a huge paycheck for a short weekend. Enough money to pay a mortgage payment or two. Yet no matter how many times she told herself it wasn't so, the money in her hand felt like payment for sex. She jammed it into the pink bag, hating the feel of the dirty money against her fingers. Fingers that had been all over Gage's body the night before.

The ironic thing about it all was that she must have been pretty good for him to pay her for another date. Well the bastard could go to hell. She wouldn't go to the charity ball with him if he was the last man on earth. And as soon as she could, she'd give that money back to him. All of it. She'd made love to him because she thought he cared about her. Her throat tightened. And she had begun to have feelings for him.

He specifically said making love to her would not imply a commitment of any type. Fiona had been a fool, and she had no one to blame but herself.

The only thing she could do now was get another job and go back to work to save the family ranch. Gage Tate could go to hell.

CHAPTER 12

MURPHY'S LAW was in full force the week before the charity ball. Nothing Gage did worked out, no matter how hard he tried. He was beginning to think he was cursed or had a little black cloud following him everywhere. The project that had only been three weeks behind now appeared to be on hold for another two weeks, pushing it five weeks behind schedule.

On the construction site, he kicked at an empty cardboard box. Though the work was in a downward spiral, it wasn't the job that had him wound up so tightly that it wouldn't take much for him to explode. It was Fiona.

He couldn't get the woman out of his mind. Everything reminded him of her and he couldn't get images out of his mind of her lying naked in his arms, smiling up at him as she ran her fingers over his body. Holy hell. There he went again, his groin tightened at the same time as heaviness weighed him down. He hadn't called Fiona since the day he'd left her at the Temptation airport, a wad of cold hard cash in her hand. He hadn't held her one last time or kissed those soft pink lips. God, he wished he'd handled that better.

His cell phone rang and he hit the talk button, recognizing the caller ID. "Hey, Coop."

"Emma tells me you screwed up, and I should call and give you a good ass-chewin'."

Gage snorted."I don't know what you're talking about."

"She ran into Britney and Bianca at Mona's beauty shop yesterday. They told her they'd shoot your ass if you showed up on the Rafter M Ranch ever again."

"What?" Gage shook his head. "Again. I don't know what you're talking about. I didn't do anything to the twins."

"Yeah, well apparently you did something to their sister and they're out for blood. Yours."

Gage scrubbed a hand over his face. "Damn. I don't have time for the drama. What is it they say I did to her? I didn't do anything but what she wanted."

"Gage, she's a woman. You probably did what she *said* she wanted, not what she *really* wanted. All I know is that you better make it right with her. The twins said she hasn't stopped crying since she got back from your weekend trip to Colorado."

A knife twisted in Gage's heart. "She's been crying?"

"Buckets of tears from what her sisters told Emma. I had to hold Emma back from coming after you herself."

"Fuck." Gage paced to a stack of I-beams and back to his truck. "I didn't mean to hurt Fiona."

"Well, you did."

"She said she wanted it to be all business."

"It's like when Emma tells me not to get her a present for Valentine's Day. It means I better get her something really nice or we won't be having sex for a month. Women don't always say what they mean."

"Then how the hell do I know what she means?"

"You have to ask her." Coop sighed. "Do you have feelings for her?"

"I barely know her. Hell, I dated Lacy for a year and thought I had feelings for her. Then she ditched me for another man. How do you know when the feelings are strong enough to do anything about it?"

Coop chuckled. "Let me ask you this. If you knew a man—not you—had hurt Fiona's feelings enough to make her cry what would you do?"

The thought of Fiona crying buckets of tears tore him up inside. She didn't deserve to be treated badly. "I'd take a baseball bat to him."

"There you have it," Coop said.

"I have what?" Gage spun in a circle, staring up at the Dallas skyline, wishing he could fly out of the disaster that was his life.

"You have it bad for her."

"But I've only known her a week." Could he be in love with Fiona McKenzie?

Coop went on, "The first time I met Emma, I knew she was the one for me."

"I don't believe in love, much less love at first sight." But he had admired her spunk and her legs in those sexy shorts when she'd served him beer at the Ugly Stick Saloon. Maybe not at first sight, but there had been a spark the first time he'd seen her.

"Then that's all there is to it. Walk away."

"Walk away? Are you out of your mind?" Wasn't that what he'd done when he'd left her at the landing strip? Coldheartedly handing her cash and asking her to pretend to be his date at another event, offering her more money to do it. Hadn't that been a slap in her face after the incredible night they'd spent together in Colorado? Hell, he'd been so confused by his own feelings, he'd stomped all over hers in what he now could see was a deliberate attempt to push her away. Afraid to invest his feelings for fear of being rejected again. If one woman could do it, why wouldn't another?

What was it Fiona had said? She wasn't like other women.

Well, hell. No matter what a dumbass he was, he couldn't stand the thought of Fiona crying over him.

"Gage, do me a favor. If Emma calls, tell her I gave you that ass-chewing. You're gonna have to figure out what it is between you and Fiona. But you better figure it out soon, or you'll have half the women in the county after your hide." Coop hung up, leaving Gage staring at the phone like it had grown horns and a tail.

He'd made Fiona cry. Fiona, the tough as nails female who'd turned him down on their first date arranged by Leslie's online dating system.

"Fuck!"

Gage punched the buttons on his phone. He had two days to make this right. Two days to put plans in place to make it up to Fiona for making her cry. Forty-eight hours to get her to the charity ball as his date, not his paid escort. His first call was to his image consultant. Haddie would know whom to call to set his plan in place. His next call was to Joe, his driver, bodyguard and private investigator. Fiona had taken the job of being his pretend girlfriend for one reason only. She needed the money. Why? Was her family in a tight financial situation? Was there anything he could do to ease their troubles?

He believed she had opened herself to him because she wanted him, not because of the money he'd paid her to go with him the previous weekend. Fiona would never take money for sex. She'd made herself vulnerable to him and he'd been an ass. If she never talked to him again, he'd understand.

His goal by the time the charity ball came around was to apologize and show Fiona what a beautiful, desirable and special woman he thought she was. Maybe, if he did it right, she'd give him another chance to prove Leslie's system had gotten it right.

CHAPTER 13

A WEEK PASSED and Fiona hadn't gone a day without thinking about Gage and the charity ball he'd asked her to attend as his fake girlfriend. Every day, she'd firmly pushed the event to the back of her mind until Saturday, the day it was to take place.

Fiona arrived early that afternoon at the Ugly Stick Saloon to help Audrey prepare for a large group scheduled for a class reunion at the saloon. The Ugly Stick owner had promised to give her twenty percent of the fee and any tips for her trouble.

Despite the hours she put in at the saloon along with the job cleaning and inventorying at the feed store in Temptation, Fiona had barely been able to pay to have her father's truck fixed. It had needed new gaskets, an alternator and spark plugs. Her brother had done all the work for free, but the parts added up.

Britney and Bianca had found part time jobs and worked in the afternoon and evenings after their beauty school classes. Britney had put together a flier for cleaning services and landed work with several businesses in Temptation. She and Bianca cleaned offices and bathrooms, helping earn the money they needed to take their state board exams.

Everything helped, but the ranch work still fell primarily on Fiona and her father. They barely scraped by with enough money to buy feed for the horses, cattle and hogs, much less pay the remaining medical bills and the mortgage payment.

The banker had been out the day before, apologetic, but adamant that if they didn't catch up on the past due payments, he'd be forced to foreclose.

Fiona could have made a dent in the past due payments out of the three thousand dollars Gage had given her so far, but she'd tucked the money in her top drawer beneath her panties and refused to touch it. She couldn't spend the money when it didn't feel right. Someday soon, she'd give it back to him. But she didn't have the cash needed for the fuel to get her to Dallas and back. And she wasn't sure what she'd say when she returned the money.

Though he'd treated her heartlessly after the most mind-blowing sex she'd ever had, she couldn't help but wonder if he'd been as scared as she'd been when she'd woken the next morning. She'd thought one night with him would be enough to exorcise him from her mind. God, she'd been so wrong. Lying in his arms all night, being close to him and feeling him move inside her had only made her want to be there always. She barely knew Gage Tate, but what she had learned about him was that he'd loved his foster parents and their deaths had been a huge blow to him.

He'd been hurt by an ex-fiancée and was probably gun-shy about jumping into another relationship. Hadn't he said making love to her didn't mean he was committing to anything? Hell, she'd thought she'd be okay with those terms.

Fiona glanced at the clock on the wall behind the bar.

"It's five minutes since the last time you looked at that clock." Audrey, her pregnant belly getting bigger every day stood beside her. "When did he say your chariot would arrive?"

"About now at the ranch." Fiona wiped the surface of one of the tables and moved to the next. "It doesn't matter. I'm not going."

The entrance door to the Ugly Stick opened and a figure stood in silhouetted against the late evening sunshine streaming through the door.

"Hey, darlin'." Gage's deep, resonant voice filled the empty bar and wrapped around her like a warm caress.

The urge to run to him and throw herself into his arms nearly overwhelmed her. What was it about this man that made her want to ignore all her misgivings, toss caution to the wind and hold him forever?

Gage stepped inside the bar and the door behind him swung closed.

As her vision adjusted to the dim lighting all over again, she noticed the bouquet of flowers he held in his arms. Deep, velvety-red roses.

Audrey nudged her toward the man. "Uh, Fiona. I believe he's here for you."

Fiona's heart thundered against her ribs and she

pressed a hand to her chest to keep it from exploding out of her chest. "What are you doing here?"

"I hoped to have a date with a beautiful woman."

Before he finished, she shook her head. "You said if I didn't show, up you'd know my answer." She frowned at him. "I didn't show up."

"I really didn't expect you to." He took a step toward her, and then another. "I was stupid."

"You were an ass," Audrey said with a smile. "I hope what you have to say makes a difference. Poor Fiona's been a basket case all week."

"Audrey!" Fiona admonished. "I thought you were my friend."

The bar owner laughed. "I am, sweetie. If he makes you cry again, I have a loaded shotgun behind the bar, and I'm not afraid to use it."

Gage grimaced. "I hope you won't feel the need to use it either. I came to apologize for the terrible way I treated you last Sunday and to ask you to reconsider coming to the charity ball with me."

"Why? So that I can pretend to be your girlfriend again? I have your money at the house. I was going to give it to Leslie to return to you. All three thousand dollars."

"I'd tell you to keep it, but I think it's what got me in hot water in the first place." He held out the roses and stared at her with those beautiful blue eyes that melted her insides. "These are a peace offering. And I really am sorry. My only excuse is that I was scared."

Fiona's heart fluttered and her knees wobbled. She forced a sorry-attempt at a snort. "You? Scared? Not likely." She turned away from the flowers and from the contrite look on Gage's face. She didn't want to forgive him. Staying mad at him was easier. Safer than opening her heart only for him to trample it again. She drew in a deep breath, squared her shoulders and faced him again. "What do you really want, Gage? You don't need a girl-friend for tonight. You can always say I'm sick."

"I want you, Fiona. Not a piece of arm candy. I deserve your anger. I know that, but I'm hoping you'll give me another chance. I want to hold you in my arms," he said, closing the distance between them, his voice lowering, caressing her with his words. "I want to feel again the way I did in Colorado."

She fought the urge to lean toward him. Instead, she lifted her chin. "Well, I don't ever again want to feel the way I did when you left me at the airport." An errant tear slipped from the corner of Fiona's eye.

Gage handed her the roses and curved one arm around her, drawing her against him. "Baby, I'm sorry."

"Now, we're getting somewhere." Audrey chuckled. "And that's my cue to leave you two alone."

Fiona couldn't pull away from the man if she'd wanted to. Her traitorous body leaned into him and she found herself inhaling the heady maleness of him.

In jeans and a blue chambray shirt, he didn't look like the billionaire he was, and he almost seemed attain-able in the darkness of the saloon. "Gage, why me? I'm way out of your league."

"You're right. You are out of my league." He brushed a stray strand of her auburn hair behind her ear. "I don't come close to deserving you."

She shook her head. "I don't know how to act in your circles. I'm just a simple country girl."

"There is nothing simple about you. You're beautiful, you have a college education, you're independent and yet you have a heart bigger than Texas."

"So why did you come tonight?"

"I came to try to convince you that you should give me a second chance. At least a second date."

She clapped a hand to her mouth. "Oh, my god, you're missing your charity ball."

He shrugged. "If I miss it, that's fine. I'll carry my cranky reputation another year."

"No. You're doing so much for the abused children. You need to be there and let them know you really care."

"I'm not going without you. If that means staying and helping you wait tables here at the Ugly Stick Saloon, that's what I'll do. To hell with the ball."

"I can't let you do that."

"The only way I'll go is if you go as my date. My real date, because I want to take the most beautiful woman, with a heart of gold, to the ball."

Fiona glanced down at the shorts, tank top and boots she'd worn to work. "I couldn't go, even if I wanted to. I'm not dressed for a ball."

Gage's smile spread across his face and he took her hands in his. "Would you go, if you were dressed for a ball?"

Her brows twisted. "Yes, but—"

"Audrey!" Gage shouted.

The pregnant owner hurried out of the back room. "Is the building on fire?"

"Audrey, can you do without Fiona tonight?" Gage asked.

Audrey smiled. "As a matter of fact, I just got off the phone with Mona. She can take Fiona's place for tonight's reunion. Fiona, go to the ball with your Prince Charming."

Fiona's heart lifted, filling her chest until it felt as though it would explode. "But the dress…"

Gage spread his arms wide. "Darlin', meet your fairy godmother." He drew her arm through his. "Your chariot awaits."

When Fiona had arrived at the saloon earlier, she'd been so depressed she wanted to find a rock to crawl under. Now, she dared to hope there could be something more than business between her and Gage Tate, the billionaire.

The limousine stood in the parking lot with Joe standing beside the back door, holding it open for her. "Ma'am."

"Joe, it's good to see you again." Fiona slid into the back seat, tugging at her short shorts, thinking they weren't the typical dress code for a limo.

"Dallas is a good hour and a half away. Assuming we find a shop open and with a gown that fits, by the time I dress and we get across town to the ball, it'll be over. It's impossible." She really didn't care. She was with Gage. The long sad week melted away in the fifteen minutes since he'd arrived.

Joe turned the limo away from Dallas and headed toward Temptation.

"Joe headed the wrong direction. Dallas is to the east."

Gage grinned. "I know."

"Don't you want to tell him to turn around?"

He shook his head. "No."

"We'll be too late."

"No we won't." A smile played on his lips.

The butterflies in Fiona's stomach whipped at her insides. What was he up to?

Joe pulled into the little Temptation airport and parked near a helicopter.

Fiona's pulse shot up. "Are we going in that?"

Gage nodded. "It's much faster than going by the highway. Twenty minutes, tops."

She chewed on her bottom lip. "Let me guess. You're the pilot."

Again, he nodded. "Or we could take the hour and half and drive to Dallas."

Joe opened the back door and held it for Gage and Fiona. "Mr. Tate is an excellent helicopter pilot," he assured her.

Fiona's lips twisted. "I should have known."

The flight took only eighteen minutes from the time they lifted off the ground to landing on the top of a high rise with a helicopter pad.

The elevator whisked them down to the ground floor where a limousine service waited outside the building.

Gage handed her in and slipped in beside her. Twelve blocks later, they pulled into the back parking lot of another building. A night watchman held a door open for Gage and Fiona to enter then led them down a long hallway and into a dark, cavernous room.

Fiona leaned on Gage's arm and whispered, "I thought we were going to the ball."

"We are." Gage said as lights flooded the room,

exposing racks of formal, designer gowns and a short row of dressing rooms. "After you choose a dress."

Two women in black uniforms stood beside the dresses, ready to assist. Within minutes they had her measured, assigned to a dressing room and stripped. One by one they brought gowns to her.

One woman stood at the dressing room door. "Would you like Mr. Tate to help you select a gown?"

Her cheeks burning, Fiona shook her head. "No. I'd rather it was a surprise."

"Good choice." The woman smiled and left to inform Gage he was not welcome in the fitting rooms.

The other assistant held a dress for her to step into. "We have a seamstress on standby to hem or fit the dress you select."

"Oh, dear, I hate to keep y'all so late on a Saturday night."

"Mr. Tate compensated us well," the woman responded as she zipped the back of the teal mermaid dress. "Let's find a dress you'll love. Then, while the seamstress is altering the gown, the stylist will do your hair."

"Stylist?" Fiona pressed a hand to her breast, her lungs locking up, and the shock of all that was happening too much for her to contain.

"Yes. Mr. Tate has seen to everything. All you have to do is decide what to wear. We'll do the rest." The woman looked more excited than Fiona, clapping her hands together as she spoke. "He's your own personal fairy godmother."

Fiona laughed out loud, her nerves releasing in a fit of giggles. What was happening felt like something out of storybook or dream. Not something that would happen to Fiona McKenzie, special education teacher, fresh out of college, who had yet to find a job teaching.

"It's too much," she murmured. He was spending too much. How would she ever pay him back? How much did it cost to have all these people on standby, after hours?

Some of the excitement seeped out of her as she stared at the beautiful teal gown in the mirror.

"What do you think?" the assistant asked.

Fiona shook her head, searching for a price tag. There wasn't one on the dress. She supposed if she had to ask, she couldn't afford it. "I need to talk to Mr. Tate." Wearing the dress, she stepped out of the dressing room and marched barefooted through the fitting area into the lounge beyond.

Tate stood with his back to her. When he heard the rustle of her dress, he turned and smiled. "That's beautiful."

Fiona shook her head. "It's too much. I can never afford to pay you back for even half of what you're spending. Dresses, hair stylists, helicopter rides." She threw her hands in the air, her eyes filling with tears.

"Hey, hey." Gage slipped an arm around her and pulled her close, tipping her chin up, forcing her look him in the eye. "I'm doing penance."

"But you don't have to." She touched his cheek. "You already apologized. That's enough for me."

"Maybe for you, but I wanted to do this. If not for you, then for me. Please. If it makes you feel better, consider it part of my attempt at improving my image."

"How does pampering me improve your image?"

He brushed his lips across hers, making her forget her question with the spark of emotions zinging through her system. "I will have the most beautiful woman on my arm at the ball."

Fiona opened her mouth to protest, but he pressed his finger to her lips before she could.

"Knowing that you are the most beautiful woman inside as well as on the outside will be what keeps me from leaving early or saying something to one of the rude elitists who always show up to these events. It's no secret, I detest society events. I throw this ball for the children, but normally I don't attend. My image consultant insisted I go this year to prove I'm not an ass." He kissed her again.

"You're not an ass." Fiona kissed him back. "Well, not always."

"Look," he said. "If you don't want to go to the ball, I'll take you to a nice restaurant, we'll have our first real date, and I'll be perfectly happy to have you all to myself."

Fiona chewed on her bottom lip for a moment. "If we go to the restaurant, you won't have to spend all this money on a dress, stylist and everything else."

"Sweetheart, these people will get paid whether or not you make use of their assistance."

With a deep breath in, Fiona realized, no matter what, the money was spent and Gage still needed the public appearance to improve his image. "If we go to the ball, do we have to stay long?"

"Only until midnight. Then I can take you home..." His mouth hovered over hers, his breath tickling her lips. "Or, my apartment is only a block away from the event. Your decision, but I'd love to hold you in my arms again. Like I did in Colorado. For that matter, we could go back to Colorado tonight, if you want."

Fiona shook her head, smiling. "You're too much. I'll go to the ball with you. I'll let you know about afterwards." She ducked her head, heat filling her cheeks and other places farther south. Spending the night in his apartment...Hells bells. Just the thought made her panties wet.

Gage kissed her long and slow, sliding his tongue over hers in a gentle, passionate caress, a promise of what was to come later. Then he set her at arm's length and raked her with his gaze. "So, is this the dress?"

Fiona laughed. "It's pretty, but no."

He turned her around. "Then hurry back in there. I have to show you off at the ball." His slap on her ass sent her toward the fitting rooms.

A smile on her face, her body still humming with the heat generated by being close to Gage, Fiona entered the dressing room and got serious about choosing the dress. They didn't have much time if she still had hair and alterations to complete.

The younger assistant met her, carrying a dress in a glorious shade of red.

"Oh, my." Fiona reached out to touch the soft, supple fabric. "It's the most beautiful dress I've ever seen and such an in-your-face, brilliant shade of red." The woman who wore this dress would have every eye on her, male or female, throughout the night. Even as she drooled over the dress, she shook her head. "I can't wear red with this hair." She shook out her auburn tresses and sighed.

"Ma'am, you have that all wrong," the young assistant said. "Try the dress. You'll see."

The older assistant, holding another gown, nodded. "No need to bring more gowns. That's the one. Mark my words."

Still hesitant, Fiona let them strip her out of the teal dress, and she stepped into the red one and pulled it up over her hips. The fabric caressed her body, hugging her curves to perfection. Like the attendants predicted, the red didn't clash with her hair at all. If anything, it enhanced the vibrant, natural highlights. "Wow," Fiona said. "You were right. This is the dress."

The two ladies circled her with critical gazes, until the older one said, "It fits you to perfection. We only have to adjust the hem and you'll be ready to shine at the ball."

Both women dropped to their knees and pinned the hem, then they wrapped her in a robe, hurried her out of the dress and called the stylist into the fitting room area.

She came with the tools of her trade: cases of makeup, brushes, curl irons and hairspray. She was followed by two other women, carrying all the things they needed to complete a manicure and pedicure. A seat was wheeled in and the women went to work on Fiona. In less than thirty minutes, her hair and makeup were perfect and she had freshly painted fingernails and toenails.

No sooner had her miracle workers cleared the room of their paraphernalia and the chair and a woman with a pincushion affixed to her wrist like a bulky bracelet entered, carrying the red dress.

Careful not to destroy the paint on her nails, the women helped Fiona into the dress and a pair of dainty high-heeled silver slippers with a crisscrossing pattern of what Fiona hoped were brilliant rhinestones, not diamonds.

The hair stylist left her hair hanging in long, loose ringlets to the middle of her back, pulling it back on one side to expose her neck.

Once she was fully dressed, she stared at her image in the mirror and nearly cried. "That's not me."

"Honey," the older assistant said. "It is you, and I might say, you'll be the most beautiful woman at the ball." She handed her a shiny silver clutch that matched her shoes perfectly and complemented her dress. It would be exactly what she needed to carry her cell phone and the two twenty dollar bills she kept as mad money, in case she needed to call a cab.

Fiona hugged the two ladies and forced herself to take several deep breaths before she stepped out of the dressing room and faced the man who'd made all of this happen. She hoped he liked the results. If he didn't, he'd have to start all over with a different woman. Fiona had never looked this good in her life and probably never would again.

Feeling like a million bucks, she nodded to the young assistant and the woman opened the door.

Gage stood on the other side, dressed in a black tuxedo with a pearl gray vest and a red rose, pinned to his lapel, the same red as her dress.

Her knees wobbled and she thought she might faint at the feet of the handsomest man in Dallas. He was a real prince charming.

CHAPTER 14

Gage had been pacing, watching the time since he last saw Fiona. Thirty-five minutes and she still hadn't come out of the dressing room. He tugged at the stiff collar of his dress shirt, wishing he could strip out of the bowtie and suit jacket and grab a beer at the Ugly Stick Saloon.

The creak of door hinges might as well have been as loud as a gunshot.

He jerked his head up and started across the room at the beauty standing in the doorframe. His heart skidded to a halt and his breath arrested in his lungs. When he his brain reengaged, he closed the distance between them.

Her gaze drifted over him and her lips parted. "Wow."

"Wow, yourself," he said. "Had I known you all the years I've been playing hooky from the charity ball, I wouldn't have played hooky."

"What?" she said through luscious red lips, shining

173

like rain-washed cherries, the corners curling upward in a hesitant smile.

Gage wanted to pull her into his arms and kiss those lips until all the lipstick faded away. "On second thought, I would have skipped every one of them to spend time alone with you." He gripped her hands in his. "We don't have to go to that ball, you know."

"No, we don't," she whispered, her green eyes flashing heat he could feel all the way to his core.

The older dressing room assistant gasped.

The youngest frowned. "Sir, you *have* to go to the ball. Ms. McKenzie will outshine all others."

Gage's cell phone rang, threatening to jerk him out of the trance Fiona had thrown him into.

Fiona laughed. "Aren't you going to answer that?"

"Answer what?" he said, staring down at her.

"Your phone."

Reluctantly he pulled it out of the inside breast pocket of his tuxedo and groaned at the name displayed.

Haddie Madison.

He started to put the phone back into his pocket.

"It's okay. Answer it," Fiona encouraged him.

He hit the answer button, regretting answering the call already.

"The ball started over an hour ago. When will you be here?" Haddie demanded.

"We'll be there in fifteen minutes," he responded, although reluctantly.

"Thank god. I have the press here, waiting to get pictures of the host and his date. The guests are all excited that you will be here and they can't wait to see who you're bringing." She paused. "By the way, who is it you're bringing?"

"You don't know her, but she will be the most beautiful woman at the ball."

"Fabulous!" Haddie said. "Now get your tukus over here before the press starts making up lies about you."

Gage ended the call and tucked his phone into his breast pocket. "That was my image consultant. She's insists we hurry it along."

Fiona thanked the ladies, hugging each before she allowed Gage to lead her to the exit.

"Since the ball is only two blocks away, we should be there in less than fifteen minutes," he said as the door closed behind them and they stepped onto the wide sidewalk.

"Fifteen minutes to go two blocks?" Fiona asked. "We could walk it in less time."

"Woman, you insult me," he said, winking. "I will not have my date arriving with her hair windblown and with aching feet after hoofing it two blocks to the ball." He waved his hand at a man positioned at the corner of the building. He, in turn, waved and a moment later, a white horse appeared, pulling a white carriage. The driver wore a black suit with a matching top hat.

When the carriage pulled up next to the curb, Gage glanced at Fiona, his brows rising. "Too much?"

She smiled and shook her head. "It's perfect. I'll be Cinderella going to the ball."

"Only there is no wicked stepmother to spoil your night." He handed her up into the carriage and climbed in beside her. The horse took off at a gentle pace.

If Gage had his way, they'd drive right past the hotel

where the ball was taking place and continue on to the building where he lived.

All too soon, the carriage arrived at the front of the hotel. The driver climbed down and opened the carriage door.

Gage got out first and wrapped his hands around Fiona's waist, lifting her out of the carriage and lowering her to the ground in front of him. He bent to brush her cheek with his lips. "It's funny how that dress looks so good on you that it makes me want to rip it off and make love to you the rest of the night."

"In front of your guests?" Fiona chuckled, the sound so sexy, it made his cock harden beneath the smooth black trousers.

"Thank goodness, I'm not into sharing," he muttered, willing his hard on to go away

She touched his arm. "Since we're here, maybe we should make an appearance."

"If you insist." Gage patted his pocket and frowned, "But wait. No woman is fully dressed at one of these events without her accompanying jewels. Or so my buddies, Sean, Tag, Max and Coop would tell it." He pulled a long slim case from his pocket and opened it to reveal a diamond necklace and matching drop earrings.

Fiona reached out to touch the stones, pulling her hand back as if it had been burned. She pressed her silver clutch to her breast like a shield. "Please tell me those are rhinestones."

He lifted the necklace off the velvet and unhooked the clasp. "I don't think Harry Winston makes necklaces out of rhinestones, darlin'."

Fiona held up a hand, shaking her head. "Too much

was when you flew me into Dallas aboard your helicopter. This would be taking it too far over the top for me. I can't accept these."

"Then consider them on loan for the night."

"But—"

"The press will be here, ready to describe everything you wear in minute detail. Let them have fun with it."

Her brows furrowing, Fiona slowly turned. "Okay, but as soon as this is over, they go back in that box and you can take them back to where you bought them or keep them for yourself."

She lifted her hair out of the way, while he settled the necklace around her slender neck, pressing a kiss at the curve of her shoulder. Then he handed her the matching earrings and stood by while she put them on.

When she straightened, he offered her his arm. "Shall we?"

WITH HER HAND firmly tucked into the crook of Gage's elbow, Fiona walked into the massive hotel foyer, decorated with sparkling crystal chandeliers.

Lights flashed in her eyes and she backed a step, startled.

Gage put an arm around her waist and held her close. "I'm sorry, I should have warned you the press would be taking pictures."

"I'm okay. They just surprised me." Unsure of how to pose for photographs, Fiona tried to remember television images of celebrities at red carpet events and how they stood in their long gowns. She laughed beneath her breath. Who was she kidding? No one would be looking at her when Gage was the man of the hour, the billion-aire who looked amazing in a tuxedo. Hearts would be broken tonight.

A woman in her late forties pushed her way through the press. "Mr. Tate, I'm so happy you finally made it. The members of the press will be allowed exactly ten minutes to take pictures and ask questions. Then they will be asked to leave so that you might enjoy your evening." She faced Fiona, her stern look softening. "Hello, I'm Haddie Madison, Mr. Tate's consultant. You must be Fiona."

When Fiona reached out to shake the woman's hand, she was engulfed in a hug.

"You don't know how happy I am he found a date. I was beginning to wonder if he ever would." She straightened nodded to the necklace around her neck. "And he has excellent taste in diamonds. Harry Winston?"

Fiona nodded. Before she could say anything to Haddie, reporters shoved microphones in Gage's face and hers, asking questions so quickly, Fiona could only smile and let Gage answer for her. It was so over-whelming she almost had a panic attack.

The strength of Gage's arm around her waist anchored her and kept her from turning and running out the door. At exactly the ten-minute mark, Haddie herded the reporters out of the building.

Fiona dared to take a breath.

Gage bent to whisper in her ear, "Ready to go to the ball?"

"After that, I'm ready to face a firing squad." She squared her shoulders.

"Darlin' that's the way I feel about these events." He led her through the foyer into the grand ballroom.

"Gage, darling." An older woman with white hair and big, blue diamonds surrounding her throat immediately stepped forward.

"Mrs. Freemont," Gage raised the woman's hand and pressed a light kiss to her fingers. "Thank you for making this event the success it always is."

"Don't be so modest. I spent your money to make it happen. You're the star of this show, and think of all the good you're doing for the children. Oh, and let me be first to thank you for actually making an appearance this year. Many people were beginning to wonder if you truly existed." She turned to Fiona. "And who is this vision in red?"

Gage made the first introductions in what turned out to be a long line of introductions. By the time Fiona shook hands with what felt like everyone in the huge ballroom, her wrist hurt and she needed a drink.

A lull in the crowd of people around them allowed Gage to ask, "Want a drink?"

"Whiskey, if they have it," she said.

He glanced around, his brow wrinkled. "Will you be all right on your own?"

"I'm not the celebrity here. You are." Fiona's gazed around the room for the first time. "If you want something to drink, you better hurry. There are more women headed your way." She tipped her head toward a blonde and a raven-haired woman, dressed to the nines and headed their way, aiming for the richest, handsomest bachelor in the Texas.

"Thank you for the warning. Don't let them chew

you up and spit you out." He kissed her temple and ducked toward the bar in the corner.

As the young women got closer and noticed Gage heading the opposite direction, they frowned as one. The dark-haired one in the center spotted Fiona and her eyes narrowed.

Recognition dawned on Fiona.

Priscilla Langley.

Too late to follow Gage, Fiona pretended to scan the crowd, shifting her gaze away from the trio, while keeping an eye on them in her peripheral vision.

Unfortunately, since they hadn't caught Gage, they must have decided she was the next best target and descended on Fiona.

"Fiona, dear." Priscilla held out her hand. "I'm surprised to see you here."

Fiona turned a tight smile on Priscilla and gripped her hand in a firm shake. When she let go, she wanted to rub her hand down the side of her dress. Shaking hands with the raven-haired beauty was like shaking hands with a cold fish. "Hello, Priscilla."

William Langley's beautiful but horribly spoiled daughter let a sly smile cross her face. "You're not from around Dallas, are you?"

Her instincts telling her Priscilla was not her friend made Fiona hesitate before answering. "No, I'm not."

"Let me guess," Priscilla continued, "you're from some small town outside of the city and you're probably a waitress or a teacher."

Fiona stiffened, her chin rising. "Actually, I'm both."

"Ha!" Priscilla turned to the blond with the big nose. "See, Martha. I can spot her kind a mile away."

Martha laughed with Priscilla.

Her hackles rising, Fiona asked, "And what is it you do for a living, Priscilla?"

She looked down her nose at Fiona. "I don't have to get my hands dirty, cleaning up after someone else or babysitting someone's brats."

Fiona shook her head, the animosity fading to be replaced by pity for the woman. "I feel sorry for you."

Priscilla's brow wrinkled. "Why would you feel sorry for me? I have everything I ever wanted. You're the one who's probably as poor as a street bum. How did you get that dress and those diamonds? Did you sleep with Gage so that he would buy them for you? Surely you didn't pay for them yourself."

The anger returned in full force, her cheeks burning with the effort it took not to rip the bitch's head off. "No, I didn't sleep with Gage for the clothes I'm wearing or the jewels, not that it's any of your business. I might work for a living, but I prefer it that way. I appreciate what I do have more and the relationships I've developed with the people I work with. I also appreciate my family, not for what they can give me, but for who they are. I enjoy giving my love, my time and my effort to making others happy."

Priscilla snorted. "That's what poor people say."

"Priscilla!"

Fiona didn't know when William Langley joined them. He appeared at Fiona's side, a scowl slashing across his forehead and his cheeks a mottled red. "Priscilla, my dear, I've had more than enough of your bad temper and disrespect for others. Go home."

"But, Daddy," she pouted, "I'm over twenty-one. You

can't tell me what to do. I'll go home when the party is over."

"If you know what's good for you, you'll go home now," he said, his voice low, threatening. "Your days as a freeloader are over."

"What?" Priscilla's eyes widened. "You can't mean that, Daddy. I'm your only daughter."

"And I've done you a huge disservice pandering to your every whim. Well, I'm done with that."

The woman blew air out her nose like a bull preparing for the fight. She faced Fiona. "You! This is all your fault. If you hadn't come along and spoiled every-thing, I'd be with Gage tonight and Daddy wouldn't be mad at me."

"I can guarantee you would not have been with me tonight." Gage handed Fiona a glass filled with amber liquid and ice. He had one of his own. "Did I miss something?"

"Nothing important." Fiona took the glass and tipped it up, downing the liquid in one long swallow, the fiery alcohol burning a path to her belly. Not that she needed it to bolster her courage. Her red hair and hearty Scot-tish ancestry stood her well when confronted by bratty students or spoiled heiresses.

Gage's presence was welcome, giving her at least one person in the room full of hoity-toity society people on her side. His strength and sheer size made her feel safe and protected.

William Langley shook hands with Gage. "Tate, good to see you. Miss McKenzie was just schooling my daughter on proper manners and priorities. Priscilla is on her way home."

His daughter pressed her lips together and stomped her foot. Then she spun on her Jimmy Choo heels and marched from the ballroom, her blond friend hurrying to keep up.

Mr. Langley turned to Fiona and took her hand in both of his. "Please accept my apologies for my daughter's poor behavior. I spoiled her too much after her mother's death. Believe me when I say I have the utmost respect for people who work for a living, no matter what they do. It takes all jobs to keep this big old world of ours turning."

"Thank you, Mr. Langley. Priscilla didn't bother me. I'm not ashamed of being a waitress or a teacher. I love both jobs and the people I have the privilege to teach and serve."

Langley smiled at her and looked over her head at Gage. "You most certainly have a keeper in this young lady. And for the record, I've kept you hanging long enough. If you still want the property on the corner of Griffin and Elm, I'll have my lawyer get with your lawyer and draw up the documents." The two men shook hands again and then Langley left them to greet an acquaintance.

"You did it." Fiona set her glass on a nearby table and turned to squeeze Gage's arm. "Langley loves you."

"No, I believe he has a thing for one gorgeous redhead who has a way of telling his daughter what he wishes he'd told her a long time ago." Gage set down his glass and gathered Fiona's hands in his as the string quartet in the corner of the ballroom played a waltz. "Haddie informed me that everyone would be waiting for us to lead off the dancing. Would you consider dancing with me? I'm not all that graceful, but I can be deeply grateful for someone who has the patience to put up with me."

"I'd be honored." Fiona stepped into his arms, and he waltzed her around the center of the dance floor.

Like everything else he did, he was an excellent dancer, leading her with a firm hand on the small of her back, making every move seem natural and perfect.

"Is there anything you can't do?" Fiona asked, smiling up at him as the music ended.

"I can't make time pass quicker. Will midnight never get here?" He glanced at the watch on his wrist and groaned.

Loud tapping sounds banged through the speakers. "Ladies and gentlemen, may I have your attention please?" Mrs. Freemont, wielding a microphone, stood on the dais with the string quartet. "We'd like to thank Mr. Gage Tate for sponsoring the annual charity ball to benefit the abused children of Dallas and surrounding areas."

"What is that woman up to now?" Gage muttered.

The room erupted in applause.

She went on to name others who'd been involved in the planning of the event and the amount of money they'd collected thus far through private contributions and the high price tag of the tickets to attend. "Now, we'll have a few words from our sponsor, Mr. Gage Tate, Texas's most eligible bachelor. Although, it appears he might not be on the market much longer."

Fiona's cheeks flushed with heat. She stayed put on the edge of the dance floor.

"Please, excuse me." Gage squeezed her hand briefly and then joined Mrs. Freemont on the stage.

A smile pulling at her lips, Fiona watched the man she suspected she was falling madly in love with give a speech. From what he'd told her, Gage would rather have every tooth in his head pulled than get up and talk in front of a bunch of people he didn't know.

"I don't know what you did to get him up in front of an audience. Lord knows, I never could convince him it was in his best interest." A woman with rich chocolate hair stood beside her wearing a silvery dress that shimmered with handsewn beads and rhinestones.

Fiona chuckled, casting a glance around the room, noting that everyone was staring at Gage, giving him their full attention, because he was interesting, not because he was a billionaire. "He says he doesn't like crowds, but they love him."

"He never did realize how important it is to build a network to help him expand his business interests."

A frown pulled at Fiona's forehead. "I'd say he's done pretty well expanding his business." She shot a glance at the woman beside her and asked, "Who are you?"

The gorgeous brunette held out a hand. "Lacy Welch. Gage's fiancée."

Fiona's fingernails dug into the silver clutch as she fought not to use it to slap the woman silly. This was the idiot who'd heartlessly dumped Gage for a wealthier man. "Don't you mean ex-fiancée?"

She shrugged. "I could have him back whenever I want him."

"Really?" Fiona forced a laugh. "That's not how I

heard it. How did he describe you? Oh, yes, as the bullet he dodged."

The stunning brunette's lips thinned. "Did he tell you that to get you into his bed? Trust me. He'll tell you anything to get into your panties. But when he gets ready to settle down, he'll come back to me. I belong in his world." The woman raised her brows as if to say, *And you don't.*

Her words struck a cord with Fiona she couldn't deny. Everything Lacy said had sounded like the ramblings of a jealous bitch, except the part about Fiona not belonging in Gage's world. If his world was society parties and spoiled heiresses, Lacy was right. Fiona would never fit in and she didn't want to.

"You should get out now, before he breaks your heart," Lacy said.

Her chest tight, Fiona stared at the man on the stage, speaking to a crowd of people who were far above Fiona's social sphere. He was charming, well-spoken and seemingly comfortable addressing them.

"Do you want me to call you a cab?" Lacy pushed. "Why embarrass yourself any more than you already have?"

Fiona wasn't listening to Lacy, her mind moving forward to tomorrow. When the ball was over and she returned the jewelry and the dress, where would that leave her with Gage? He'd made no commitment past this night. She hadn't asked for one.

Her hand trembled and she stared down at it, her vision blurring. She'd miss him so much. Then her hand shook again and she realized her phone was vibrating in her clutch.

"I can have one of the waiters show you to the door and hail a taxi for you," Lacy offered.

"Shut up." Fiona opened the catch for the clutch and pulled her phone out.

She had five missed calls from home and three text messages, the latest one with only three numbers.

CHAPTER 15

HER FAMILY WOULDN'T HAVE LEFT that message or called that many times knowing where she was and whom she was with unless it was a dire emergency.

"Gage will never love you like he loves me," Lacy was saying.

"Lacy, Gage doesn't love you and never will," Fiona said, as she dialed her home number and pressed the cell phone to her ear. As she waited for it to ring, she glared at the woman. "Grow up and move on." Taking her own advice, Fiona walked out into the lobby of the hotel, away from the music and crowd.

The phone rang five times and no one answered.

She glanced at the time. Midnight. Why wasn't anyone answering the home phone at midnight?

Her heart banging against her ribs, she dialed Bianca's cell number and waited.

Her sister answered on the first ring. "Fiona, thank God."

"What's wrong? Are you okay? Where's Britney?"

"Britney and I are okay."

A heavy weight sank into Fiona's belly and her throat closed, refusing to let her ask what needed to be asked.

She didn't have to. Bianca spoke, her voice shaking, "It's Dad. He's had a heart attack."

CHAPTER 16

Gage made it through the presentation, hitting every one of the points Haddie had prepared in a speech she'd encouraged him to memorize. He hadn't needed to, knowing how important it was to raise money and public awareness for the plight of abused children in their community. When he was wrapping up with the final comments, he glanced across the room to where he'd left Fiona. Her red dress captured his attention, making him want to finish with the formalities and take her away to his apartment where he'd make love to her for the rest of what was left of the night.

In the morning, he'd start all over. Perhaps he'd order food to be delivered so they wouldn't have to leave. He would show her a hundred different ways to make love and then he'd make up a few new ones to keep it fresh.

He wrapped up his speech and was about to step down from the stage when Mrs. Freemont waylaid him to present a certificate of appreciation to him. That's when he spotted his former fiancée standing beside Fiona.

Gage's fists clenched. What was Lacy up to? The woman had moved on to a man wealthier than he had been two years ago. Since then, Gage had gone on to build his reputation and bank account to top even Lacy's new sugar daddy's status and financial stability.

Surely she wasn't feeding Fiona a load of crap to scare her away from him? Anxious to keep Lacy from spreading lies, Gage tried again to leave the stage. This time, the mayor of Dallas stepped up to present the key to the city to him for his contributions to the charity.

Haddie stood to the side of the stage blocking him from leaving before every goddamn person in the room had an opportunity to thank him. When he finally broke away, dodged Haddie and the well-wishers, Fiona was no longer where he'd left her.

"If you're looking for your date," a feminine voice said, "she left."

Gage turned to face Lacy, a smug expression on her face.

He gripped her arms and said through gritted teeth. "What did you say to her?"

"Nothing but the truth." She smiled. "That woman will never belong in our world. She wouldn't be happy and neither would you. You need someone who fits in and knows who's who and can enhance your career and social network."

His fingers tightened on her arms until she frowned and squirmed. "Ouch, you're hurting me."

He let go of her and said, "You lying, venomous b...." Gage bit down hard on the word he wanted to call her, realizing it would do no good. Lacy and Priscilla were so much alike. Spoiled, with an inflated sense of their worth. "Stay away from Fiona, and stay the hell away from me."

"Oh, Gage, honey, don't be so mean. I only did it for your own good. I love you and only want the best for you."

"You only want the best for *you*. There's no one in the world more important to you than you."

"You have it all wrong, baby. I'm sorry I walked away from you, but I'm back. We can be together. I'm the right woman for you. You and I belong here in the city, among these people."

Gage stared at her wondering what he'd ever seen in her. "Lacy, you're deluded. There is no you and I. I don't belong in Dallas high society. I only tolerate it because I have a business to run. If you've messed things up between Fiona and me, I will find a way to make your life even more miserable than you make it yourself."

He spun and hurried out of the ballroom, pulling his cell phone from his pocket as he left. He had to find Fiona and fix whatever had happened to make her leave, because one certainty stood out above all else—Fiona was different from all the women in the ballroom. She didn't have to tell him for him to realize it, and he was more certain than he'd ever been in his life that he loved her and would do anything to make her his. It might take time, but he'd do it.

≈

TWO WEEKS after the ball and the horrible night in the

hospital, Fiona stood in the living room of their modest home, smiling at her father as he slept in the lounge chair, having fallen to sleep watching one of his favorite John Wayne movies.

Her father had been transported to the Dallas hospital via the Temptation fire department's ambulance. She met Bianca and Britney in the emergency room. Shortly after Fiona had arrived, her father had gone through several tests to determine he had considerable blockage in his heart, and he was lucky to be alive. The doctor told them he wouldn't live much longer unless he had bypass surgery.

Fiona and her sisters had been in the room with her father when the doctor delivered his news. They'd all unanimously agreed, he had to have the surgery to restore the flow of blood into and out of his heart.

Just as they wheeled Fiona's father into surgery, Gage arrived taking her into his arms and there she'd stayed.

"What's happening?" he demanded.

Fiona filled him in on the little bit of information she had.

Gage took charge. He asked questions and made phone calls, arranging for the leading heart specialist in the country to be on call if the doctor performing the surgery ran into any difficulties.

The next few hours had been the longest of Fiona's life. After losing her mother and stepmother, she wasn't ready to lose her father, too. She huddled in the waiting room with her sisters and Gage, alternating between pacing and praying. Not until the doctor emerged to tell them her father had come through surgery did Fiona finally breathe deeply. It would take time for him to recover, and he wouldn't be able to work on the ranch.

With the medical bills mounting up and no chance any of them could manage the ranch without their father's help, Fiona came to the conclusion it was time to let go.

The ranch might have been in the family for over two hundred years but, to Fiona, it didn't mean anything without her father.

Gage stayed by Fiona's side through the next few days until her father was released from the hospital. He arranged for transportation to get him home and for everything they might need to make him as comfortable as possible during his recovery. He'd even had someone in to repair the floors and replace the hot water heater. Fiona didn't know how or when, but she'd pay him back.

Once the McKenzies were home, Gage returned to Dallas, saying he'd be in touch soon. Fiona hadn't seen or heard from him since.

She didn't have time to stand around crying, so she went to work getting her family's lives in order.

As soon as her father was recovered enough to discuss what was next, they made the decision to sell everything but the house and a few acres around it.

Thinking it would take a long time to find a buyer who wanted to purchase over twelve hundred acres, they were all shocked when within a week of putting it on the market, they had a buyer willing to pay full price in cash for lock, stock and barrel.

With the worry over money resolved, Fiona went to work getting her own life in order.

Since she hadn't seen Gage, she figured he didn't need her anymore. Unfortunately, she still needed him and wanted him to be a part of her life. The week he'd been around helping her through her father's illness, she'd grown to rely on him and appreciate having him close. He was kind and teasing with her sisters and gentle with her father when he'd been moved to the house. For a while, she'd thought he care about her and her family and would be around.

Then a week had gone by with no word from him. At the end of that week, with Lacy's words echoing through her head, Fiona stood staring into her closet at the beautiful red gown, knowing it had all been a dream. She never would fit into that world, nor did she really want that life. She loved her family and living in the country, away from the traffic and drama of the big city.

Fiona gathered the dress, shoes, clutch, necklace and the three thousand dollars Gage had paid her and took them to Emma. She promised to have Cooper take them to Gage the next time he saw him.

As the days passed, Fiona missed Gage more, the pain in her chest growing deeper instead of fading. She didn't have the luxury of crying. With her dad out of commission, it was up to her to be the rock in the family. And though the ranch had sold, they still had the few animals they'd kept, including two horses, a handful of chickens and a barn cat. Fiona took care of them and worked at the saloon in the evenings.

Bianca and Britney had been a mess. It was all Fiona could do to make them concentrate on their work and their state board exams.

Fiona prayed they were doing well. They'd left that morning for Dallas to take the exams. Fiona would have gone with them, but she didn't feel comfortable leaving her father alone yet. Thankfully, she would be home for another six weeks before school started. She'd been interviewed and selected for the position of special education teacher at Temptation's elementary school. Soon she'd have a classroom full of children with special needs. Though she should be happy, she found it harder and harder to smile. What was wrong with her? She would be going to work doing what she'd always dreamed of and her father had made it through one of the biggest challenges of his life and lived.

Selling the ranch hadn't even hit her as badly as she'd thought it would. Not seeing or hearing from Gage for over a week hurt the most.

Fiona wandered out onto the porch and sat in one of the old rocking chairs. Because she didn't know how soon her sisters would be back from Dallas, she'd told Audrey at the Ugly Stick Saloon, she couldn't work that night. She wouldn't leave her father alone. He and her sisters were all the family she had left. Fiona had no intention of squandering any time she had left with them.

She'd just settled in the rocking chair and was staring out at the land that would no longer belong to the McKenzies when the whop-whop sound of rotor blades disturbed the tranquility.

Her heartbeat kicked up and she stepped down off the porch, shielding her eyes against the brilliant sunshine.

A sleek black helicopter lowered to the ground in

the pasture, startling the few cows chewing their cud in the shade of an old oak tree.

Fiona stood in the grass, her insides trembling as the blades came to a complete stop. A man stepped down from the craft and plunked a cowboy hat on his head. There was no mistaking the sexy swagger of the guy who'd been on her mind every hour of every day since she'd last seen him.

GAGE TATE CROSSED THE FIELD, swung his legs over the rail fence and dropped to the ground, his gaze on Fiona every step of the way as he closed the distance between them. When he stood in front of her, he took her hands in his. "Hey, darlin'."

She shook her head, tears welling in her eyes. "Don't 'hey darlin' me."

He slipped his hands around her waist, having dreamed of doing that and a whole lot more for the past week. "Miss me?" "No," she said, the tears trickling out of the corners of her eyes.

His heart bunched tight in his chest at the sight of those tears. He hated that he'd made her cry, and at the same time, it gave him hope that she really cared.

"Well, I missed you." He wiped a tear from her cheek and brushed her hair back behind her ear.

She sniffed, her bottom lip trembling. "You had a funny way of showing it."

His heart lighter, he fit her hips to his and leaned his forehead against hers. "I had some projects I had to work."

"Did you get them done?"

"Almost," he admitted.

"I suppose you'll be leaving soon, then."

"It depends," he said, kissing the tip of her nose.

Her breath hitched and she reached up to trace the line of his jaw, her gaze seeming to drink him in.

In her T-shirt and faded cutoffs, wearing no makeup whatsoever, she was the most beautiful woman he'd ever seen. "I'm sorry I was gone so long. I had some thinking to do, and I knew I couldn't be objective with you around, so I made myself leave, even when I wanted to stay more than anything."

"Did you come to any conclusions?" she asked, her voice a halting whisper.

He nodded, lifting her hand to his lips. "Life is too short to get hung up on some things."

"Like what?"

"Like the fact we've only been on two dates and only known each other a total of three weeks." He couldn't resist kissing the curve of her neck or the sensitive place beneath her earlobe.

Fiona leaned her head to the side, giving him better access to kiss her. "Who's getting hung up on that?"

"I was. You see, I don't believe in love at first sight. It just can't happen."

"It can't?" she drawled, standing on her toes to kiss his chin and neck.

"No. But I've also come to the conclusion that Leslie's software was one hundred percent accurate in choosing my perfect mate."

She reached up to brush back the lock of dark hair that had fallen over his forehead. "And you came to this conclusion when?"

"When I was signing the papers for the purchase of this really great homestead that had been in the previous owner's family for over two hundred years."

"What?" Fiona leaned back to stare into his face. "Please don't tell me you were the mysterious buyer who paid cash at the sale?"

"Okay, I won't tell you," he said grinning. "The problem is, I have all this land and I don't have time to manage it. I can hire ranch hands, but they need someone to tell them what to do. I was hoping your father, when he's up to it, could work for me as my foreman."

She blinked eyes shining with unshed tears."Why?"

"Well, there's this girl." He frowned. "No…woman… with gorgeous red hair and amazing green eyes that I'm head over heels for, but it might take time to convince her I'm on the up and up. I want to give her all the time in the world to get to know me and what a nice guy I can be, with the right woman."

More tears welled in Fiona's eyes and she swiped at them. "You didn't have to buy my ranch to get me to agree to go on another date with you."

"No, but I wanted to buy a ranch that would be a great place to start a family and raise kids." He smoothed his hands over her shoulders and down her arms to her wrists. "Do you like children?"

She nodded, butterflies flapping their little wings in her belly. "I do."

He let out a long pent-up breath. "Enough to have a couple of them?"

Her cheeks turned red and she murmured, "It depends."

"On?"

"Who I'd be having them with." She cupped his cheek in her hand. "He'd have to be willing to live in the country, want at least half a dozen kids and be up to helping out when it comes to changing diapers. I have a job too."

His throat tightened. "I know a man who meets those qualifications."

"Are you sure he would trust me not to walk out on him when given a better offer?"

"You keep telling me you're not most women." His face split in a grin he couldn't hold back a moment longer. "Baby, I believe you."

She smiled. "You might just work out."

"That leaves only one thing to do."

"What's that?" she asked.

"To seal the deal with a kiss." Gage drew her close.

"And here I thought fairytales were for dreamers and silly girls." She threaded her hands into his hair and clung to him. "But here I am, in the arms of my very own Prince Charming."

"I'm no prince," he said, pressing his lips to hers. "But you're definitely my perfect match." Then he crushed her to him, devouring her in a kiss that sealed the deal and his heart.

THE END

Enjoy other books by Elle James

Billionaire Online Dating Service
The Billionaire Husband Test (#1)

The Billionaire Cinderella Test (#2)
The Billionaire Bride Test (#3) TBD
The Billionaire Matchmaker Test (#4) TBD
Texas Billionaire Club
Tarzan & Janine (#1)
Something To Talk About (#2)
Who's Your Daddy (#3)
Love & War (#4)

TARZAN & JANINE

TEXAS BILLIONAIRE CLUB BOOK #1

New York Times & *USA Today*
Bestselling Author

ELLE JAMES
&
DELILAH DEVLIN

TARZAN
&Janine

NEW YORK TIMES BESTSELLING AUTHORS
ELLE JAMES
DELILAH DEVLIN

CHAPTER 1

"Holy Hell." Tanner Peschke groaned.

"My friend, you worry far too much." Rip O'Rourke grinned from across the table but stared through the barroom door.

Tanner rolled his eyes. Rip didn't look as though he had a care in the world—the eye-straining Hawaiian shirt paired with his beat-up cowboy hat pretty much reflected his whole outlook on life.

"Wow, T-man. You couldn't have picked a better place for us to meet."

"I should have known this was a set up." Tanner ran a hand through his hair and stared out into the Austin, Texas hotel lobby hosting the National Beauty Products Convention. "My old man is testing me."

Rip sighed. "This place is heaven."

"It's hell for me." Tanner waved a hand at the plethora of women—slim, curvy, tall, petite, fresh-faced, mature—and in every mouth-watering color scheme available on the planet. "Look at them. All of them. I'll never make the deal he expects."

"Tanner, why don't you just tell your father you quit?" Jesse Jordan sipped his steaming coffee.

The twinkle in his eye said he understood Tanner's predicament all too well. Although women fawned over the young Robert Redford lookalike, he didn't melt like hot wax.

"You don't need Peschke Motors," Jesse said. "You make more on your investments in a month than that place sees in a year."

"I made a promise to my mother—"

"On her deathbed ten years ago." Gage Jenkins, a no-nonsense man with a military haircut and direct stare, leaned over the table. "Dude, a lot has changed since then."

"You could buy ten Peschke Motors with your pocket change." Rip shook his head. "Hell, you could probably buy your own new car manufacturing company with the money you're making in day trading."

"That's not the point." Tanner leaned back in his seat. "Why do you work at the radio station, Rip?" Irritation tightened his throat. He turned to Jesse and waved a hand. "Why do you run a ranch supply store, Jess? And why are you still a member of the Army National Guard, Gage?" Tanner glanced around at the group. "None of us do what we do because we *need* the money."

"That's right." Rip let out a belch, followed by a grin. "Sorry."

Tanner shook his head. "We started the Texas Billionaires Club so we would all succeed."

Rip nodded. "And once we made our collective billion, we are supposed to remind each other what's important."

"Family, friends and, most important, not getting a big head." Jesse counted off, one finger at a time.

"Back to the point." Gage set his coffee mug on the table with a thump. "Tanner made a promise...to his dying mother, who is family, to stand by his father...who is family."

"That's why I called this meeting, my friends." Tanner straightened his collar. "I needed moral support and a reminder of what's important. My dad's counting on me to do this right."

"Well, soldier." Gage threw back his broad shoulders and gave Tanner his best military glare. "Get out there and make that deal."

"I don't get it." Rip's brows furrowed. "What's so hard about buying a load of used cars from an old lady?"

"He's a sucker for a sob story." Jesse shook his head, a grin spreading across his mouth. "This place is filled with women, a veritable field of land mines for our man Tanner."

"You got that right." Tanner stood, staring out at the lobby, dread filling him with each passing second.

Jesse, Gage and Rip stood, Rip leaning in like a quarterback in a huddle. "Keep your eye on the ball. Ignore the other team, and the fact you'll be surrounded and outnumbered by the fairer sex."

"Thanks," Tanner snorted. "I'm ignoring them already." His tone dripped sarcasm.

"You can do it, buddy." Rip pounded him on his

back. "Just pretend they're all men in drag and breeze right through."

"We've got your back." Jesse took his turn pounding Tanner's back. "Call us when you're done. We'll give you a cyber high-five."

"I'm on it." Tanner strode out of the bar and entered the lobby. Knowing the TBC had his back gave him fuel to get going.

On his way to the reception desk, several lovelies nodded, smiling as they passed. Others fluttered their fingers in little feminine waves—the kind that made a man's insides curl. All the while, the combined scents of their perfumes increased the dread in his sensory-overloaded brain.

Tanner cleared his throat and straightened his red tie. Time to get serious. This meeting was important to his father's business and crucial to Tanner's future at Peschke Motors. The appointment could be the beginning of bigger and better things...or the beginning of the end.

Passing a large gilt-framed mirror, he checked his appearance. He'd been shooting for honest and down-to-earth to appeal to the matriarch and CEO of Barbara Stockton's Beauty Secrets. Thus the blue chambray shirt, crisply ironed blue jeans, and highly polished cowboy boots. Next to all the beautifully groomed and fashionably dressed women in attendance at the conference, he probably looked like a hick. He got great pleasure in knowing he wasn't just a hick. He had money. Lots of money, but he chose not to advertise that fact. No one in Texas but his banker knew exactly how much money he had. And he liked the situation that way.

Tanner usually didn't give much thought to what he wore or how others viewed him, but his normally take-me-as-I-am attitude had gone for a hike after his father's latest challenge, which he'd delivered just that morning...

"Son, if you're gonna run this company when I retire, you've gotta show me you want it."

That was the hard part. Tanner really didn't want the business. He didn't have Jesse's steadiness, Gage's laser-focus, or even Rip's laissez-faire attitude. He was a man approaching thirty and feeling strangled in place because he hadn't found his life's calling.

Sitting across the desk from his father, Tanner silently groaned and tipped his cowboy hat forward so his dad couldn't detect his impatience. He knew he was in for his father's latest lecture on "Used Car Sales Business: Lecture Number 4123."

Try as he might, he couldn't force the passion his father had for the sales game. But Tanner promised his mother on her deathbed that he'd help his father with the family business. He wished he'd inherited his father's natural used-car-salesman gene. The fact was, he hadn't.

Just once, he'd like hearing his father's praise and admiration of his business prowess. But his father wouldn't sugarcoat what wasn't there for him to see at Peschke Motors.

Too often, Tanner bit hard on his tongue to keep from telling his father he didn't need him or the job or anything to do with Peschke Motors. But his sweet mother's last words always came back. "Take care of your father. Help him. He needs you."

"Tanner!" Joe Peschke's booming voice pricked the bubble of Tanner's memory. "Son, are you payin' attention to anything I'm sayin'?"

"Yes, sir," Tanner lied and decided he'd better give the man his undivided attention, or this could turn into an even longer ordeal than usual. By the look of his father's ruddy cheeks and bristling black moustache, Tanner guessed he'd missed a cue.

His dad rose to his feet, his bulky frame towering over Tanner. "I plan on buyin' a fishin' boat and a house on the beach. In exactly three months, I'm movin' there. Do you understand what I'm sayin'?"

Tanner must have drifted *way* off. This was the first he'd heard about his father moving. "You're moving?"

"Yes, I'm moving."

"But how will you run the business from the coast?"

"I'm won't. I'm retirin'."

"Retiring?" This was new, too.

"Yes, and I wanted to leave the family business in the hands of family. I had high hopes that family would be you, seein' as you're the only family I have left."

Tanner pushed his hat back on his head, every fiber of his being tuned in to his dad's words. He could feel a "but" coming...

"But, I need a quarterback who can lead the team to victory. Problem is, son, I'm just not seein' you as that quarterback."

Wait a minute. Tanner couldn't have heard that right. "You mean, you'd fire me?" he asked disbelieving. A little devil in his conscience leapt for joy, while an angel with a face like his mother's shook her head sadly.

"Not necessarily fire you, but I need to select a general manager. If you're not the man for the job, I can't put you in it."

A cold, hard lump lodged in Tanner's throat. Perhaps now was the time to break it to his father that he was a multi-millionaire and didn't need the job of general manager. But that time had come and gone. Telling his father he didn't need him might break the old man's heart and would definitely go against what Tanner had promised his mother. Caught between a rock and a soft spot, Tanner argued, "I've sold fifteen cars in the last month, Dad. How many other salesmen have sold as many?"

Joe Peschke shook his head, his mouth turned down in a sad frown. "Not a one. Volume's not your problem, son."

"Then what is?"

His father lifted a piece of paper from the stack on his desk and shook it. "Statistics show every car you sold to a woman, you sold *at*, or a fraction above, cost. Which barely pays the bills around here, much less your commission."

Tanner knew he couldn't refute his father's words. "But Dad, you don't understand."

His father shook the paper. "Then help me understand, son." Scanning down the list, he poked a finger at a line. "The green conversion van."

"That would be Mrs. Jenkins." Tanner straightened his shoulders. "Her husband's disabled and they live on a fixed income."

His father frowned and looked farther down the list. "How about that blue, four-door Saturn?"

"Rebecca Pitkin." Tanner remembered the frazzled redhead with the toddler. "Student. Single mom. Needed reliable transportation to get her daughter to daycare. She's trying to make a better life for herself and her child."

With a roll of his eyes, the older Peschke went to the next line. Crossing his arms over his chest, his father slowly shook his head. "Tell me about the F-150 Pickup."

Tanner groaned inwardly. Was this how a frog pinned to a dissecting board felt? "F-150 pickup?" Damned if he could remember the face that went with that vehicle. "Refresh my memory, Dad."

"Micky Freeland ring a bell?"

"Micky... wasn't that a man?"

"I don't know too many men who dot their 'i's with hearts."

"I could have sworn she was a man," Tanner muttered. A sick feeling filled his stomach. His father was right.

Tossing the paper back in the pile on his desk, his father leaned forward. "Truth is, son, you're a marshmallow with the women."

"And that's a crime?" Tanner knew the answer before the words left his lips.

"In the used car business, it is. We're not a charity organization." His father leaned back in his chair, pinching the bridge of his nose. "The word is out. You sold three cars to three generations of Smithson women. And they'll all be tellin' their friends."

"That could be a good thing." *C'mon, Tanner, spin this in your favor.* "Return customers and word-of-mouth advertising is bound to be good for business."

"Won't do the dealership a darn bit of good, if they're all comin' to you, son." His father shook his head, his lips tightening. "Face facts—as soon as a female feeds you a sob story, you're silly putty in her hands."

Tanner hung his head, knowing every word his father spoke was true. He was a soft touch where women were concerned. That wily Smithson grandmother had him pegged the moment they'd met.

For just a moment, he'd held her hand, feeling the parchment-thin skin and smelling the lilac fragrance she'd doused herself in. He hadn't been able to bear the thought of the elderly pensioner making high payments for the vehicle she had her heart set on. Hell, Tanner didn't need the commission. He could subsidize every one of their customers if the action didn't leave a paper trail back to his investment portfolio.

"I have no complaints about your sales volume. You need to work on your profit margin if you want to prove you have the fire in your belly for this business."

Right now, the only fire Tanner felt in his belly was the ulcer he'd earned. Despite the promise he'd made to his mother, he still resisted committing the rest of his life to Peschke Motors.

"You've got three months. Make those months count. And, son, decide what you're gonna do with your life." His father had leaned his forearms on the desk to deliver the final warning. "Don't straddle that fence—all you'll get is bruised balls."

AT TWO O'CLOCK that same afternoon, Tanner was feeling pretty bruised all right. Standing in line at the concierge's desk in the hotel lobby, his stomach still roiled at his father's words. Even knowing he had the support of his best buddies wasn't helping.

Barbara Stockton of Barbara Stockton's Beauty Secrets, or BS-Squared as he thought of her, had requested him specifically for this deal, and that he come to her. Tanner hoped like hell she wasn't Aggie Smithson's friend. This was his chance to make the deal of a lifetime. A chance to redeem himself for all the missed opportunities—if he could keep a hard-core business mind and not be swayed by a woman's woes.

"I'm here to meet with Barbara Stockton. Could you tell me what room she's in?" he asked the busy concierge.

"I'll have to call her room first to verify the appointment. Could you wait just a moment, sir?"

"Sure, I'll wait over there." Tanner pointed toward a potted plant set next to an entryway.

Women moved in surges, ebbing and flowing from the ballroom. Feeling out of place and outnumbered, he swam with the current until he reached the plant. He almost grabbed hold to keep from being swept into the sea of estrogen. More than once, he could swear he felt the soft pat of a hand on his ass.

Tanner stared into the ballroom from his anchoring tree, feeling incongruous as the only male for as far as his eyes could see. The large expanse was partitioned into dozens of booths where women demonstrated various beauty products. Hands in his pockets, Tanner forced himself to relax. He leaned against the door-frame and heaved a sigh.

Why were women his greatest weakness? What about them made him such a pushover? Every last one of them—be they homely or gorgeous, elderly or eligible—left him feeling like he had to protect them, take care of them, and ease their worries. Why did they have that affect on him, and how could he armor himself against it to pull off this deal?

He had a knack for bringing in the customers. Perhaps he should stick to publicity and marketing and let someone else handle the sales. He certainly wasn't helping the dealership if he gave away cars. And Peschke Motors had been a part of the Peschke family for three generations. The place meant a lot to his father, therefore, the business meant a lot to Tanner.

How could he make his father proud and keep the business going? Ideas raced through his head, none seemed substantial enough to impress his father.

"Please notice when Rafael applies the Miracle Hair-spray, it goes on evenly, without spitting or clogging."

Tanner heard her before he saw her. Though soft and breathy, the voice carried over the steady hum of hundreds of feminine conversations. And that voice made every hair on his body stand up and cry *halleluiah*.

Because he stood a good foot above the tallest, he didn't have to crane his neck to see over the heads of the women gathered.

A beauty perched on a stool with a mini-micro-phone attached to the low-cut lapel of her suit jacket.

"Holy hell," Tanner breathed.

When the spraying stopped, the woman climbed gracefully from the high stool and shook her hair back from her shoulders. "See? Every hair remains in place with a springy, natural hold."

Tanner's gaze remained riveted—but not only to her hair. Her entire package captivated him from the top of her golden blonde coif to the tips of her bright pink, Barbie-style stilettos. Every curve and feature in perfect proportion, her beauty was reminiscent of Marilyn Monroe. And that musical, breathy voice made his pulse flutter and his mouth dry. Tanner's blood raced from his heart to his extremities—one in particular.

The cotton-candy pink suit that would have looked feminine but professional on any other woman, clung lovingly to her generous curves. The skirt ended just above her knees—round, pink kissable knees. The three-inch stilettos emphasized delicate ankles and well-defined calves. But just her physical perfection wasn't what drew him, she dripped sweetness.

Tanner gulped and forced himself to look beyond the woman to the enraptured crowd gathering around her. With her voice, beauty and natural talent, she could sell beachfront property in Arizona. *Or...*

A Cadillac of an idea slipped into Tanner's mind and gunned all eight cylinders.

This gifted, eloquent and drop-dead-gorgeous woman could be the answer to all his prayers. But who was she?

Tanner stepped forward, but pressure on his arm stopped him, and he looked to the source.

"Excuse me, sir." The concierge stood at his elbow, drawing his attention from his salvation. "Ms. Stockton will see you now in the Double Diamond suite. It's on the forty-sixth floor—the first door on your right when you exit the elevator."

"Thank you very much." Tanner turned to treat himself to one last glimpse of the curvaceous blond in the pink suit. "I'll talk with you later," he whispered before heading for the elevator and the dreaded meeting with BS-Squared.

THE TRIP to the forty-sixth floor took only three minutes. Not much time to compose his scattered thoughts. Thankfully, the fifty-something-year-old Ms. Stockton couldn't possibly hold as much appeal as the breathy blonde who waited below. And she wasn't old enough to play to his soft side, like the infamous Aggie Smithson.

Tanner rapped lightly against the door bearing the shiny brass nameplate with "Double Diamond Suite" engraved in bold letters.

When the door opened, he turned up his smile full force. "Hello, I'm Tanner Peschke, you must be..." Tanner's voice faded and his smile slipped.

"Barbara Stockton," she finished for him. "Won't you come in?" Turning, she stepped aside and waved a hand with a flourish, indicating the way.

He gulped, and his heart sank to his knees. "I'm doomed."

"Pardon me, did you say something, Tanner? You don't mind my calling you Tanner, do you?" Barbara Stockton's throaty voice purred. She eyed him with a raised eyebrow and a knowing smile.

"I said, nice room." Edging past her, he entered the lioness's den.

For a woman in her fifties, Barbara Stockton was very well preserved. Her shoulder-length, dark brown hair curled artistically around her face and glinted with beautifully engineered red and gold highlights. She wore a full-length wrap made of a filmy leopard print. Beneath it, she sported a black sports-bra and figure-hugging leopard-print leggings. And if that wasn't enough, the black thong worn over the leggings was the clincher.

Tanner frowned. This was no Aggie Smithson. Barbara Stockton was a very astute businesswoman, a lion in the jungle of gone-by-the-wayside beauty products distributors. What did he have to fear? She didn't inspire him to one iota of protectiveness. If anything, he felt like raw meat being dangled to entice her ravenous appetite.

Pushing back his shoulders, he stood tall, schooling his face into that of a professional businessman. Tanner was sure even a seasoned negotiator like his dad would have difficulty with this feline. With a raised eyebrow, he said in his smoothest voice, "I'll wait by the window while you get dressed."

He could handle this. Barbara's beauty didn't appeal to him. But the blonde downstairs did, and he couldn't wait to return to the ballroom to propose his idea for the dealership.

"Daahhling, you seem awfully tense." Barbara's voice tickled the back of Tanner's ear as her fingers dug into the taut muscles at the base of his neck. "*Relaaaxxxx.*"

Tanner inhaled deeply, but it didn't work. How could a man relax when a cat had her claws in him?

"It's awfully warm in here, don't you think? I just finished working out." She slipped the filmy wrap from her sleek, well-toned shoulders and the garment cascaded to the floor in a careless heap. With a practiced turn, she walked toward a cabinet on the far wall. "Can I pour you a drink?"

Think blonde, think blonde. His new mantra had the immediate effect of bringing to mind the pretty spokeswoman in the ballroom downstairs. Thinking of the two women, Tanner realized no comparison existed.

Granted, Barbara Stockton was incredibly hot, but she didn't have the same impact. Her moves were too predatory, too calculated. A feral cougar, he could resist.

"Yes, I'd like a drink." Tanner eased his mouth into a genuine smile, feeling more confident by the moment.

"What's your poison?" she asked with a little flirty glance from beneath her brown eyelashes.

"Whiskey." He smiled wider, confidence restored, a feeling of invulnerability spiking his blood.

With his 'Marilyn' firmly fixed in his mind, he spent the next two hours playing musical chairs among the sofas and loveseats in the suite, while negotiating the purchase of a fleet of cotton-candy pink company cars from the equally determined CEO.

By the end of the meeting, Tanner had won. He'd gotten BS-Squared's handshake—and unsolicited kiss—on a contract that promised the dealership a tidy return once they'd repainted and sold the vehicles. The contract was a coup de grace, and he hadn't had to compromise the company, or himself, to get it.

Exiting BS-Squared's suite with a promise from her to visit the lot, Tanner allowed a little strut in his stride as he returned to the ballroom. He was determined to find "Marilyn". During his time with BS-Squared, he'd begun to think of the blonde as his good luck charm. Somehow, he had to convince her to come to work for Peschke Motors.

Once inside the ballroom, he was disappointed when he didn't see her at the Miracle Spray booth. After five minutes of scanning the multitude in the area, he finally spotted her on a raised dais, astride a mechanical bull.

She'd changed her clothing. Body-hugging denim and gray snakeskin boots were topped with a scoop-necked pale pink T-shirt that ended just above her silver belt buckle.

"As you can see, even a full two hours after applying Miracle Hairspray, my hairstyle is still in place."

Tanner was fascinated. He hadn't imagined the sexy, breathy voice. Nor had he exaggerated the impact of her voluptuous figure. She spoke with the confidence of an experienced actress and, even more intriguing and definitely arousing, she rode the mechanical bull like a pro.

With a hand gripping the rope tied around the torso of the beast, she held her other arm high in the air in true rodeo-rider fashion. Each rise and fall caused the woman's breasts to lift and dip. That little space of skin between her tiny T-shirt and her belt played peek-a-boo with her audience.

God Bless America—and the inventor of the mechanical bull. Every red-white-and-blue blood cell in Tanner's body rode south. Without thinking, he crossed the ballroom floor and climbed onto the dais. He had to talk to her now.

"EVEN A BUCKING BULL can't destroy the beauty and natural spring." Janine Davis recited her scripted lines without fail. Maybe this wasn't an Academy Award-winning performance, but she gave it her all anyway. Every acting job added a credit to her resume, putting her one step closer to realizing her dream.

"Ma'am, I don't think the hairspray has anything to do with your beauty."

The voice from behind startled her into forgetting her lines and temporarily losing her balance. The bull dipped, and she started to slip. She dropped her arm and grabbed the rough hemp rope encircling the bucking bull.

When she'd righted herself, she glared at the tall man at her side. "Please don't talk to me, sir."

"What if I have a question about the product?" he countered, a smile curving his mouth.

Taking another dip, she loosened her grip and pressed her free hand to the microphone on her lapel. "I have a script to follow, and you're not in it. Please don't distract me," she whispered fiercely, loud enough for him to hear, but not for other conventioneers passing by. She forced a bright smile, directing it toward the audience.

"Pardon me, ma'am. I wouldn't dream of keeping you from your job."

Her gaze narrowed, but he didn't appear to be mocking her. "Good. Now please move along before you get me fired." Janine scanned the room full of people, looking for her boss, before returning her gaze to the man beside her.

He was kind of cute. Tall and dark with a grin that could melt a girl's bones into a gooey puddle. He spread his large hands wide, an innocent look on his smiling face. "Now, how could I get you fired? You're positively brilliant."

Exasperated by his persistence, and at herself for getting all tingly when he was near, she replied, "All I know is I need this job to make my rent money, so don't blow it for me."

"All right, but first tell me your name." He leaned back against the bull's control panel and crossed one ankle over the other.

The man's brown-black eyes held a wicked gleam she found hard to resist. "Janine Davis. Why do you ask?" she said, fighting hard not to notice how sexy he was because the bull's rhythmic motions jounced her breasts and drove her lower parts hard against the saddle. Sensations she had no business noticing began to build along with the thrumming heat flooding her veins.

"I wanted to know the name of the woman I need to thank."

Curiosity won out. Her annoyance at his interruption forgotten for the moment, her head tilted to the side as she continued rocking back and forth on the bull. "Thank me? Why?"

"Because of you, I made the best deal imaginable with old BS-Squared herself."

"Who's BS-Squared?" she asked.

"Barbara Stockton of Barbara Stockton's Beauty Secrets. You know—B. S. B. S..."

Janine frowned.

"Two BS's is BS-Squared." He shook his head. "Never mind. You're my new good luck charm. I just made the best deal of my career."

A movement behind the gorgeous cowboy caught Janine's attention, and her heart nearly stopped. Her boss was headed her way. With her hand squashing the microphone to her breast, Janine whispered, "Uh, sir, don't look now, but..." She jerked her head in his direction.

He ignored her attempt to interrupt and continued, "So you see, I have you to thank for keeping my mind on business with old BS-Squared."

Janine cringed. Why hadn't he taken her hint and shut the hell up? She let go of the rope around the bull's middle and waved, pasting a smile on her stiff lips. "I wouldn't thank me now," she sang.

"Why?" The tall man's eyes widened and his jaw slackened. His gaze locked with Janine's. "She's right behind me, isn't she?"

"Uh huh." Janine nodded. "Uh...hi there, Ms. Stockton." She bit the corner of her lip and fluttered her fingers in a strained attempt at a light-hearted greeting.

The cowboy swung around, his elbow knocking against a lever on the control panel.

The bull leapt into high speed.

Janine squealed and grasped for the rope—for something to hold on to—but her hands flailed uselessly in the air.

After three raucous bucks, the bull spun, knocking

the man from the stage to land flat on his butt on the floor in front of Barbara Stockton. At least he'd earned his just desserts.

Janine smirked and would have clapped her hands if she weren't in trouble herself. The bull jerked one direction, then lurched and spun another, flinging Janine through the air.

She screamed and twisted, attempting to land on her feet. Instead, she fell face-first on top of the man who'd caused all this.

"Ooomph!" Their chests met with enough force to knock the wind out of them both. Stunned, and fighting for her breath, Janine resisted the urge to hide her face against the cowboy's broad chest. She wished a gigantic black hole would open up and suck in her humiliated self.

Unfortunately, Janine felt the intensity of her boss's glare before she pushed up on her hands and turned to smile sheepishly. "See? The hairspray holds even through the worst of conditions."

Ms. Stockton's expression was not amused. "My, my, isn't this touching. The hired help flirting with the used car salesman."

Janine had a gut feeling the tightness on the older woman's face did not bode well. Turning her anger to the cause of this debacle, she glared down at the man lying beneath her.

WHEN JANINE LOOKED down at Tanner, all he could think about was her thighs straddling the only unstunned part of his body. Her full, rounded breasts pressed intimately against his chest.

Barbara Stockton's outraged expression didn't even faze him when Janine struggled to sit up. He could feel himself harden in response to her denim-covered bottom rubbing against his groin. How much torture could a man take and survive?

A clicking noise next to his ear finally got his attention. The sound was a shoe tapping against the floor— Ms. Stockton's shoe. When his gaze made the trip up the long sleek legs of his client to rest on her angry face, his stomach plunged.

"This whole scene reeks of low class. And I make it a habit to deal only with high-class operations..." BS-Squared's eyebrows rose as she stared pointedly at him, then turned to Janine, "...and individuals. I'm afraid your services are no longer required, Miss Davis. Collect your wages and get out of my sight."

"But Ms. Stockton—" Janine pushed to a sitting position astride Tanner.

A pretty little frown making her even more adorable in Tanner's books.

The CEO held her hand up. "Just leave."

A wad of guilt twisted in Tanner's gut.

"And, Mr. Peschke?" BS-Squared's lips moved with careful, cutting precision. "The deal is off." Executing a perfect about-face, she left the room and the disaster Tanner had created in her wake.

Tanner groaned and let his head flop back against the floor, welcoming the slight pain. His dad was going to kill him.

"Thanks for nothing, mister." Janine finally got her feet beneath her and rose.

Tanner stood and flashed a scowl at the crowd gathered around them, and they quickly dispersed. He turned to Janine. "I'm sorry about that. Hitting that switch was an accident."

"As far as I'm concerned, you're a walking accident looking for a place to happen." Her words were clipped and angry. "Now, what am I going to do? This was the best-paying acting job I've had in a while."

That was his cue. If he wanted to keep his good luck charm, boost profits and do it his way, he had to convince Janine to go along with his plan.

Brushing off his hand against the side of his leg, he held it out. He gave her the smile his grandmother had told him could *tempt the birds from the trees*. "Janine Davis, have I got a deal for you."

ABOUT THE AUTHOR

ELLE JAMES also writing as MYLA JACKSON is a *New York Times* and *USA Today* Bestselling author of books including cowboys, intrigues and paranormal adventures that keep her readers on the edges of their seats. With over eighty works in a variety of sub-genres and lengths she has published with Harlequin, Samhain, Ellora's Cave, Kensington, Cleis Press, and Avon. When she's not at her computer, she's traveling, snow skiing, boating, or riding her ATV, dreaming up new stories. Learn more about Elle James at www.ellejames.com

Website | Facebook | Twitter | GoodReads | Newsletter | BookBub | Amazon

Or visit her alter ego Myla Jackson at mylajackson.com
Website | Facebook | Twitter | Newsletter

Follow Me!

www.ellejames.com
ellejames@ellejames.com

ALSO BY ELLE JAMES

Engaged with the Boss

Cowboy Brigade

Time Raiders: The Whisper

Bundle of Trouble

Killer Body

Operation XOXO

An Unexpected Clue

Baby Bling

Under Suspicion, With Child

Texas-Size Secrets

Cowboy Sanctuary

Lakota Baby

Dakota Meltdown

Beneath the Texas Moon

Made in the USA
Las Vegas, NV
04 July 2024